I0545093

Brooklyn

The Adlers

By

Avery Gale

BROOKLYN
Copyright © 2018 by Avery Gale
ISBN: 978-1-944472-73-3
Print Edition

ALL RIGHTS RESERVED: This literary work may not be reproduced or transmitted in any form or by any means, including electronic or photographic reproduction, in whole or in part, without express written permission.

All characters and events in this book are fictitious. Any resemblance to actual persons living or dead is strictly coincidental.

PUBLISHER
Avery Gale
averygale.com

Dedication

As an author I've discovered inspiration comes from all directions and often from the most innocuous appearing interactions.

That was the case with the ending of *Brooklyn*.

An innocent question from a loyal reader and good friend about a baby's gender, changed the ending of the book in a huge way.

If you get a giggle from of the chaos at the resort, join me in thanking **Loretta McGaughey** for asking the perfect question!

The Adlers

The siblings... their occupations, and ages at the beginning of the series:

Austin – 31 – CEO of the family oil conglomerate based in Austin, TX.

Asia – 30 – Ruthless legal eagle for the family business.

Bronx – 29 – Owns a string of car dealerships in partnership with brother, Cleveland.

Cleveland – 28 – Race car driver.

Brooklyn – 27 – Retrieval expert for big insurance companies.

Catalina – Freelance intelligent agent working with the CIA, MI6, Mossad, and others. Travels the world as a successful jewelry designer.

Israel – Security expert and tracker.

Kensington – Actor.

London – Chemist.

Paris – College student.

Watch this page for updates in subsequent books in this series.

Chapter One

BROOKLYN SLID EFFORTLESSLY down the rough-cut rock wall of Emilio Mendoza's palatial home. The jagged granite was the only part of the enormous structure not facing the pounding waves of the ocean. The man's legendary paranoia led him to choose a nearly perfect location, but his ego was even bigger than his obsessive fear, and he'd overplayed the hand by installing a sub-par security system.

Proving her point, Brooklyn patted the small package secured in a well-concealed pocket along her thigh. She silently wondered what it would be like to have enough power and money, you felt it was your God-given right to steal anything you coveted, knowing law enforcement wouldn't touch you. Not only had the locals refused to move against Mendoza when insurers insisted he'd stolen the priceless artifact, they'd actively impeded federal and international agencies' efforts as well. *Un-fucking-believable.*

The sound of waves pounding against the rocky shore and the low howl of wind whipping through the palms was oddly soothing, but as any experienced cat burglar will tell you, those comforting sounds could also mask a multitude of dangers. Anything that hid the telltale signs the norm was no longer in place was a threat. As much as she appreciated the hypnotic sounds of the surf, Brooklyn tried to focus on the underlying sounds around her.

Keeping to the shadows and moving slowly, her black Lycra® jumpsuit not making a sound as she slid soundlessly through the night, Brooklyn sent up a silent prayer of thanks for her younger sister's brilliance. London Adler's *Whisper Spray* had been an enormous blessing.

As a research and development chemist, London had immediately understood the problems Brooklyn outlined, describing the sleek fabric's tendency to be too noisy for the new sound-sensitive security systems. Six months later, London sent a bottle of spray that turned out to be a game changer. *Having a kid sister who was an upcoming star in the pharmaceutical industry definitely has its perks.*

Bringing her thoughts back to the present, Brooklyn wondered why men like Emilio Mendoza stole artifacts, then locked them in vaults rather than allowing their beauty and rich history to be shared with the world. She understood the monetary value of the ancient, solid gold Egyptian amulet, but if you couldn't have the bragging rights of ownership, what was the point? *And why the hell would anyone keep something so precious in a safe manufactured while Woodrow Wilson was president?* Smiling to herself, Brooklyn wondered if her high school history teacher had any idea how valuable his lesson on Wilson's implementation of safe standards had been.

"If you're going to stash something of such significance and value, you should at least have a decent security system and vault. You should invest in something that doesn't belong in a museum, asshole." Realizing she'd muttered the words aloud, Brooklyn froze mid-step for several seconds.

Damn it all to dancing dolphins. She only talked to herself when she was teetering on the edge of exhaustion. Even worse, she only made mistakes when she was overly tired, and fuck Freddie Foreplay, she knew better than to push herself so far. Brooklyn had retrieved four artifacts in eight days, on three continents, and the worst part was, she didn't understand why she felt the need to push her mind and body beyond all reasonable limits.

Despite being as fit as she'd ever been, Brooklyn was dead on her feet. The few hours' sleep she'd gotten on the long flight from Paris to a neighboring island hadn't been enough to erase a week without a full night's rest. The only time she'd ever come close to being caught during a job was early in her career... before she'd learned the importance of only working when she was well-rested, and here she was pushing herself when she knew better. *Not so bright, are you?*

Born in Brooklyn, she was the fifth of ten Adler offspring, all named after the city where they were conceived. *Oh yeah, try explaining that to your friends in junior high. Nope, nothing embarrassing about being forced to admit all the places your parents bumped uglies.* What sounded like a snort sounded from Brooklyn's left, causing her to go stock still for several long seconds. Before she realized what was happening, her vision was starting to blur, and Brooklyn had to remind herself to breathe as she swayed on her feet. She might have been named in the same way as her siblings, but Brooklyn was the only one who tapped danced on both sides of the law... something she probably needed

3

to rethink if those pesky black dots ever moved out of her view.

Brooklyn Adler frustrated law enforcement officials at every turn and was on *The Most Wanted* lists in more countries than she'd even stepped foot in... a fact she continually found completely baffling. As a master of disguise, Brooklyn laughed to herself each time she slipped into countries where her picture hung on the customs' office wall. The only person she knew who was better at morphing into someone else was her sister, Catalina, who had her own reasons for needing to disguise her appearance.

Making her first million two weeks after her eighteenth birthday, Brooklyn had racked up fifty more in the years since. She might be the bane of law enforcement agencies' existence, but she was the beloved golden child of insurance companies all over the world. She'd long since passed the point where she no longer needed to work, and despite what some people might believe, she wasn't still working for the money. Hell, it wasn't even about the rush of adrenaline more powerful than any drug. It was simply about being the best and setting right at least a few of the many things wrong in today's world.

LUKE GRAYSON LEANED back against the smooth rock wall surrounding the Mendoza estate and sent up a silent prayer he had enough time to get Brooklyn to safety before the storm brewing offshore wreaked havoc with his well-laid plans. He had no intention of being trapped in a hidey hole on this small island with Brooklyn Adler during a damned tropical storm. The only thing he'd ever known the tiny bundle of stealth to be frightened of was thunderstorms—and they rendered her virtually helpless.

Watching as Brooklyn slipped silently down the wall, Luke wondered if she'd sensed the shift in the weather because he saw her foot slip on one of the irregular stone blocks, causing her to reach wildly around her for something to hold on to. The damned woman was usually poetry in motion, but she was definitely off her game tonight. They'd been friends since their freshman year in college, and even though she knew he was a gifted empath, Brooklyn had no idea how deep his connection to her had become over the years.

Opening his mind, Luke felt a wave of fatigue crash over him. The sensation was so intense, Luke worried his knees were going to fold out from under him. Brooklyn's exhaustion piled atop his own was staggering. He'd been awake almost continuously since the first hit lit up his laptop like a fucking Christmas tree three days ago. It was the first ping hitting one of dozens of alerts he'd set up on both the regular and dark webs.

At first, the information about Brooklyn was sketchy—referring to her abstractly enough, he'd wondered if he was simply being paranoid, but as other users began interacting, it became more and more obvious he'd been right. The final post referred to her as BB, a tag name she'd gained after her first retrieval when someone at the insurance company she'd worked for let it slip a *beautiful burglar* had retrieved the missing golden mask, saving his company a multi-million-dollar payout.

5

The company she was working for tonight had a leak—no, it was more than a leak, it was a fucking blowout. Somebody had sold Brooklyn out by mentioning she'd be recovering the amulet. Whoever was chatting was obviously unconcerned they'd essentially signed her death warrant. Despite the distance between them, Luke had immediately opened his mind to hers, and as soon as he knew the details of her next job, he'd shut down the link. If there was one thing he'd learned about Brooklyn in the years since they'd become friends, it was how spooked she could become if she thought he was listening in on her thoughts.

Tonight, he kept the link open long enough to send her a subtle warning and direct her in his direction. Luke smiled when he thought about how annoyed she'd be to learn he could push suggestions into her mind. Before he could fully retreat from the link, he felt her fear a split second before a dark presence steamrolled into his mind. Brooklyn was only a few feet from him, but he didn't dare shift positions to get closer for fear more movement would attract attention.

Brooklyn was moving so slowly, he wondered at times if she was moving at all. Watching her creep forward at a snail's pace when the breeze rustled the palms lining the enormous house was as fascinating as it was frustrating. The moon was playing a dangerous game of hide and seek, threatening to give away her position at any moment. Back tracing the malevolent energy, Luke was finally able to spot the men lurking in the brush.

The seconds that followed were some of the longest and most terrifying of Luke's life. He'd heard the members of the Prairie Winds teams talk about how time slowed during a crisis, but he'd never fully believed their descriptions. Opening his mind to the men searching for Brooklyn, he knew as soon as they raised their weapons despite not being able to see them. Both men saw her at the exact same moment, the separate retorts of their guns virtually indistinguishable.

Pulling Brooklyn against his chest, he felt her jerk in his hold as a white-hot streak of searing pain bled from her mind into his. The fiery burn lashed her upper arm as another tore into the flesh of her upper thigh. Wrapping his arms around her, Luke pulled Brooklyn back into the small alcove leading to the gate he was certain she'd been planning to use. The heavy metal gate reminded him of those found in old cemeteries and monasteries depicted in the old movies the two of them used to binge watch on cold New England weekends while in college. *Jesus, what's up with my fascination with movies all the sudden. Fucking focus on getting the hell out of here. There will be plenty of time for classic movies when we get to New Mexico.*

Chapter Two

BROOKLYN KNEW INSTINCTIVELY who'd grabbed her, she'd recognize the scent of his cologne anywhere. She'd caught a whiff of it sliding down the rock wall and almost lost her footing. When it passed, she decided it had been her overactive imagination. *It's a good thing he's a kick-ass computer nerd because he'd make a damned lousy thief... that woodsy scent was like a damn calling card.*

Her fatigue-fogged brain didn't register the distinctive pops of small caliber handguns firing simultaneously until someone lit her shoulder on fire and her leg folded out from under her. If Luke hadn't already had his hands on her, Brooklyn knew she'd have fallen face first onto the rough-hewn stone walkway.

"Luke? Why are you here?" She wasn't sure why she'd asked a question she already knew the answer to. He'd come to help. He was always there when she needed him. Even when she was too stubborn to ask him, he always seemed to appear, offering whatever assistance he could. Her entire world tilted dramatically to the left, and suddenly, she felt like she was floating in a turbulent sea of darkness. Warm lips pressed against her forehead, so gently, she wasn't sure if it was real or wishful thinking.

"It's real, baby. It's always been real."

LUKE SMILED TO himself as he melded back into the darkness with Brooklyn cradled in his arms. He knew she wasn't seriously injured, but that didn't mean he wasn't anxious to make his way down the steep steps leading to the rocky shore. He'd still have a couple hundred yards to get to where he'd hidden the boat before they could get the hell out of Dodge.

He could feel the amulet in one of the hidden pockets of her sleek body suit and wondered if Mendoza appreciated the real significance of the solid gold talisman he'd just lost or if his interest was simply about money. How could anyone discount the stories passed down generation to generation, hinting at the solution to one of history's greatest mysteries? Code-breakers had only recently made headway in their efforts to decipher the amulet's cryptic inscription. Whether the small golden treasure held the key to finding one of the most sought-after religious artifacts of all time remained to be seen.

"I heard shots, is she alright?" Cooper Hicks' voice was crystal clear, the communication device he'd pushed deep in his ear canal ensuring he could hear everyone else on the team. The question didn't surprise him. After all, Cooper had worked as a spook for too many years not to have been able to distinguish between the crack of lightning and distant gunfire.

Several days ago, when Luke realized how much trouble Brooklyn was in, he'd not only alerted his current employers, he'd also called her oldest brother. At thirty-one years of age, Austin Adler was one of the youngest CEOs in the oil industry, but nothing stood in his way when it came to his siblings. While Luke flew to Boston, Austin coordinated with both Kent and Kyle West, who headed up the Prairie Winds team of covert operators and called in Alex and Zach Lamont's ShadowDance team as well. In Luke's opinion, you had to respect any man who doesn't blink at the prospect of giving orders to four of the most alpha men Luke had ever met.

Alex and Zach Lamont's team of operatives was based on ShadowDance Mountain outside Climax, Colorado. Even though the two former Navy SEALs were well known for sharing leadership duties with members of their own team, neither Alex nor Zach was particularly fond of letting go of the reins when other teams were involved.

Kent and Kyle West, their counterparts in Texas, had similar leadership styles though the Wests were somewhat more relaxed than the Lamonts. Kent and Kyle enjoyed a more laid back Texas vibe, but they still maintained strict control over their ops. Luke had been working for the Lamonts for almost a year—he'd enjoyed his time there even though his original contract was to consult for six months.

A variety of incidents over the past six months had kept him on board, but he was looking forward to finding something more challenging than implementing technology to help the Club's security team keep track of their bosses' wild child wife. It wasn't that he didn't like Tobi West because he did. Hell, everybody he knew loved Tobi, but the woman was exhausting. *It's no wonder she has two husbands. Hell's bells, it takes two men to manage the team assigned to keep up with her.*

Refocussing his attention on the petite woman in his arms, Luke tapped the small lapel mic, enabling him to give the team a quick update. He hadn't sensed the shooters since the moment they'd drawn their weapons, but that didn't mean they weren't behind them.

"She's been hit, upper thigh and what feels like a graze on her shoulder."

"Cat's already on the phone with McGregor. If anyone can help us fly under the local's radar, it's Ian." Catalina was Brooklyn's younger sister, and as Luke had recently discovered, Cat and Cooper had a rather unique love-hate relationship. Luke had laughed when Brooklyn called their dance of pseudo-annoyance foreplay, and after watching them interact during the boat ride from the mainland, he was convinced the two intelligence agents were on a collision course. Whether they ended up killing one another or fucking each other blind remained to be seen.

"You think too much. I can practically hear your mind spinning, and I'm not up to your speed at the moment." At first, Luke wasn't sure if Brooklyn had spoken the words aloud or if he'd simply heard them echoing through her mind.

"Shh, sweet B, we're almost to the boat. We'll rendez-vous with the larger craft anchored offshore, then we'll see what tricks Ian McGregor has up his sleeve for getting us out of here and you to a medical facility." He felt her stiffen but ignored it. Brooklyn Adler was the most stubborn woman on the damned planet—she hated accepting help of any kind even from her family. Referring to her by the nickname only he and her family used had been deliberate. Luke wanted her settled, and he wanted her compliant, so he'd use any trick he could.

Keeping to the shadows slowed his progress down the rocky beach, but he wasn't going to risk stepping out into the open. The traitorous moon loved Brooklyn Adler and would no doubt take any opportunity to shine down on her. She'd always sworn being born under a full moon was more of a curse than a blessing. *Considering her line of work, she's probably right.*

Reaching around, Luke was able to pull the tight cap from her head. Watching the long waves of raven colored silk tumble into the breeze made him long to see soft curls draped over his bare thighs. He was tired of waiting for Brooklyn to come to her senses and admit the chemistry between them, and he was damned tired of being relegated to the friend column. She belonged to him—she had since their freshman year at MIT. They might have bonded as lab partners, but their friendship quickly became soul deep.

Visiting each other's families during holidays and sharing a house with several other students meant they'd been inseparable until graduation. Rather than looking forward to completing his college education, Luke had dreaded graduation because he'd known they'd be separated for the first time in five years.

At first, he and Brookly had talked daily, but as their respective careers took off, those calls became more and more infrequent. Even though Luke could open his mind to hers anytime he wanted to, it wasn't the same as the easy banter that had become the mainstay of their daily interactions.

Luke had the perfect opening to reconnect with Brooklyn a few months ago when Cooper's sister, Lakyn was targeted. Lakyn's apartment was just down the street from Brooklyn's in New York City, and with her background, she was the logical choice to find out whether or not the apartment had been compromised. She'd been happy to help, even discounting her usual rate in exchange for the cutting-edge technology she found in the apartment.

Brooklyn had always loved gadgets, and spy tools were her personal favorite. Knowing Ian McGregor was involved in her rescue was probably the only reason she wasn't fighting Luke tooth and nail—the pint-size techy aficionado wouldn't dream of passing up a chance to reconnect with one of the most admired inventors in the world. McGregor and Luke's uncle, Mitch Grayson, were longtime business partners, holding several joint patents.

"Thinking. Too much thinking... again. Does that brilliant mind of yours ever take a break?" Luke almost laughed out loud at Brooklyn's reprimand—he'd spoken those same words to her more times than he cared to think about. Hearing her throw them back at him after what she'd just been through was reassuring.

"Nice to know your sense of humor is still intact. Hang on, baby, we're almost there. The boat should be just around the next outcropping of rocks. How about you make sure your next island job has pristine, sandy beaches and an airstrip capable of handling something larger than a fucking drone?" He felt her smile before she slipped back into a peaceful state of unconscious bliss. As concerned as he should have been she'd lost consciousness again, he wasn't worried because he sensed her need for sleep was a bigger factor than her injuries.

Damn, baby, you are going to start taking better care of yourself. Hell, maybe I'll just tie you to my bed. Now there's an idea that has some serious merit.

Chapter Three

FIGHTING THE URGE to throw his phone against the wall, Emilio Mendoza looked up into the questioning eyes of Ian McGregor. They might be standing across the room from one another, but it was easy to see his host's curiosity had been piqued, and drawing McGregor's keen attention didn't bode well for Emilio gaining his cooperation. Of course, now it was a moot point until he got the damned amulet back.

How the hell had his team allowed the thief to slip through their fingers? What the hell was he paying them for? Two of his best men swore their shots hit the dark figure disappearing into one of the many recesses in the rock wall surrounding the compound, but they hadn't found anyone. Obviously, whoever managed to circumvent his security system knew their way around electronics—which in this day and age could be any damned kid with a game system and internet access.

A large part of his frustration was rooted in the realization he was a victim of his own false sense of security. Emilio should have known someone would eventually make a play for the amulet, it was too valuable to simply be forgotten. Time had a way of ensuring people let their guard down, and that was exactly what he'd done. It had been almost a year since he'd orchestrated the heist of the small gold artifact, so he should have known the large insurance payout would be enough to motivate the corporate bigwigs to find a way to retrieve it. Truthfully, he wasn't as interested in the piece itself as he was the coded information it was said to contain. What he hadn't expected was how long it would take to gain an invitation to one of Ian McGregor's parties.

Schooling his features, he grabbed a flute of champagne from a passing waiter and nodded in his host's direction. Emilio needed McGregor's expertise to open what he suspected was a hidden primer for the directions to a much larger prize—a prize mankind had been searching for since the days of the Old Testament. He didn't want the Ark of the Covenant for its historical significance, and God only knew he was too superstitious to open it. No, he was only interested in selling it to the highest bidder, something that would likely make his faithful Catholic mother's head spin on her shoulders.

Ian McGregor was brilliant, but he was damned hard to get close to. The billionaire entrepreneur/inventor had apparently become even more reclusive after marrying a woman who'd tried to sneak on the island. Rumor had it, striking up a conversation with Callie McGregor was the key to meeting her husband. Apparently, Ian McGregor didn't leave his lovely bride unattended with a man he didn't know for more than a couple of minutes.

Moving randomly around the outer edge of the room, Emilio made his way slowly toward where Mrs. McGregor was holding court with several other women. The group was standing beside an enormous buffet table, their relaxed body language indicating they were all friends.

Knowing McGregor's wife had designed and set up the resort gave him the *in* he needed to strike up a conversation with her since he was in the beginning stages of planning a resort of his own on a small Carribean island. His resort would have a completely different purpose, but he wasn't going to share any of those dark secrets with anyone.

IAN WATCHED EMILIO Mendoza move in a deliberate but meandering path toward his beautiful wife and submissive. The man had been angling for an invitation to a party at the resort for months so the irony he'd finally been successful the night Brooklyn Adler relieved him of the Egyptian amulet wasn't lost on Ian.

Jace Garrett, McGregor Holdings' Head of Security and Ian's best friend stood beside him, watching the man as closely as Ian. Jace had been Ian and Callie's third until he and Gage Hughes, another member of the McGregor security team, found Holly Mills. Gage was currently standing a few feet from where Callie, Holly, and friends stood chatting. Obviously, Mendoza hadn't done his homework, or he would know they never left their wives unguarded.

"Your guest didn't look happy when he ended that call, but he recovered quickly when he noticed you were watching." Jace's low chuckle belied his distaste for Mendoza. As usual, Jace's background report had been detailed down to what the man ate for breakfast every morning—it had also thrown a lot of warning flags in the air. Hell, his desperation alone had been enough to red-flag him.

Ian watched Jace tap his earbud, the man's expression not giving away anything, so Ian simply waited. Once he'd murmured his understanding, Jace gave the small electronic communication device another quick tap as he seemed to relax.

"Catalina's sister is being treated on board and will be airlifted to Evan Monroe's private clinic in Bronxville as soon as they dock."

Ian had heard of the pricey New York suburb but had never visited the area. He knew Dr. Evan Monroe had an ultra-private clinic there, and his medical, as well as his reputation as a Dom, were impeccable. Evan was a Club Isola member, and Ian had never heard anyone speak ill of him—something that was damned rare, considering Club Isola's proximity to Washington, D.C., a city that seemed to criticize anyone and everyone.

"She's got a graze on her upper shoulder and took a shot to her upper thigh that may have broken the bone. Not life threatening, but she'll be out of commission for a while."

Ian nodded and wondered where Luke Grayson would take the young woman to keep her safe. Personally, he thought the Adler sisters were in some perverse competition to see which of them could make the most enemies before their thirtieth birthday, but he'd only shared his opinion with Jace.

Luke was the nephew of one of Ian's close friends and

business partners, so he hadn't hesitated to step in and help when Mitch called to fill him in on what was taking place off the Boston shore. When Catalina called an hour later with a similar request for help, Ian had been able to tell her everything was already in place.

"Ian you are a wonder—our next collaboration is on the house." Catalina's promise warmed his heart, and Ian already had something in mind. Cat Adler was a world-renowned jewelry designer, and even though she used it as a cover to enable her to work as a contract intelligence agent, she was still damned talented. "I don't know how you managed it, but I assure you, my entire family is in your debt."

Before Callie came into his life, Ian would have been immune to the emotion he'd heard in Catalina's voice, but his sweet *Carlin* changed all that. The nickname he'd given Callie the night he and Jace caught her sneaking onto the island was appropriate, she truly was a warrior in so many ways. Turning his attention once again to the other side of the ballroom, Ian watched his wife turn to Mendoza when she realized he'd spoken to her. Her body language was screaming suspicion despite Ian's certainty her verbal response had been polite.

He watched her closely and knew Jace was doing the same. When he saw the first of her *tells*, his feet were moving before his brain had fully registered her response. Callie wasn't as gifted as either Mitch or Luke Grayson, but she was still an empath with impeccable instincts, and the shudder he'd seen move up her exposed spine spoke volumes.

"You're playing right into his hands, you know." Jace's

words were unnecessary. Of course, Ian knew Mendoza was using Callie to reel him in, but protecting his wife—the woman who'd entrusted herself into his care—was more important than avoiding the man whose desperation alone was enough to earn Ian's distrust. It was time to make it clear to Emilio Mendoza precisely where he was in the pecking order.

Chapter Four

BROOKLYN'S SWEET DREAM that her college crush was carrying her along the beach was interrupted by a shrill scream, and her entire body jerked in response. The fires of hell stabbed her upper thigh, pulling her fully from the dream she didn't want to abandon.

"Damn it, Cat, tone it down. You startled her and flinching has to be damned painful." Luke's voice was pitched low, but his frustration was unmistakable. Dancing flower fairies, how much of her dream had been reality? Brooklyn heard the splashing of water, and when she finally managed to lift her lashes, she realized Luke was carrying her to a boat anchored several yards off-shore. When he started to hand her off to another man, she wrapped her arms tightly around his neck, refusing to let go. Luke's hold on her tightened for a few seconds before he tipped his head down and whispered against her ear.

"It's okay, baby, Cooper is helping us get on the boat. We need to get the hell out of here." She shook her head, and he sighed. "The men who shot you have finally decided to track us, sweetness. We need to be out of range before they catch up, and they're closing in fast." When she reluctantly loosened her hold, a second set of arms lifted her from the safety of Luke's embrace, and she shivered at the loss.

"Hang on, Brooklyn, we'll have you settled and be on our way soon. Be a doll and let your sister fuss over you for a bit, okay? It'll keep her from wanting to drive the damned boat, and I think you know why that thought gives me nightmares." Brooklyn felt herself relax, knowing the man holding her wasn't a total stranger if he knew about her younger sister's penchant for speed. "It's a short trip out to the larger boat, but it's going to be a rough ride—the storm is closing in fast."

Cooper had no sooner uttered the word *storm,* and all hell broke loose around them. Brooklyn wasn't sure what was the most frightening... the gunfire or the lightning. Despite the white-hot lance of pain shooting through her leg, she launched herself out of Cooper's arms. She only managed two steps before her knees folded out from under her. She'd have face planted if she hadn't caught herself on the edge of one of the small craft's seats.

There wasn't time to process the pandemonium taking place around her as the boat's engine roared, jerking the boat forward with so much force, she slid the rest of the way to the floor. The hull slammed against the churning waves, knocking the air from her lungs, causing her to cry out in pain. Before she could pick herself up, Brooklyn was blanketed by a heavy, warm body. *Luke.*

"Stay down, B. Hopefully, we'll be out of range soon— unless the crazy bastards have more firepower than we suspect."

Brooklyn relaxed at Luke's use of the single initial only he and her family used as a nickname. At six foot two, Luke dwarfed her, his broad shoulders and well-muscled physique making him look as if he'd be more at home on a grid-iron than in front of a bank of computer terminals. He had to be holding the majority of his weight off her because she could still breathe. She felt him chuckle and mentally rolled her eyes, knowing his gift was even more enhanced by close body contact.

"My connection to you may be stronger when we're touching, but we both know it has been gaining strength since the moment we met. My link to you is so much more than the sum of its parts—and I think it's time we stopped dancing around what we both know would be explosive between us." Before she could respond, the boat's motor slowed, and she felt the telltale thump as they pulled alongside a larger vessel.

LUKE RELUCTANTLY LIFTED himself from Brooklyn's heat and immediately felt bereft at the diminished connection. His cock protested the slight fading of their link as much as his soul. It wasn't until he had her back in his arms, he felt the world was once again set right.

The fear he felt rolling through her wasn't from the asshats shooting at them—hell, no that would be too *normal*. Her fear of storms trumped everything else that had happened in the past half hour, and it fascinated as much as terrified him she was more afraid of the weather than the hail of bullets volleyed at them from the rocky shore.

He'd loved pressing his body against hers despite the

fuckers firing bullets and splinters of shattered fiberglass slicing his back. Damn it all to hell, he was going to be sore, and he hated blood—anybody's, it didn't matter who it belonged to. It wasn't that he was comparing his minor injuries to Brooklyn's, he wasn't—but damn, he hated the sight of blood.

Luke sighed in frustration. He hated medical people fussing over him, and why the hell did you always end up in more pain after they finished *fixing* you? His mom had preached his complaining was falling on deaf ears and continually reminded him she didn't want to hear about any accident that didn't involve first responders or surgeons. He'd learned at an early age to avoid any injury where his mom would angrily try to superglue gashes closed—the damned woman was a menace with any kind of adhesive.

Stepping from the small speedboat onto the yacht's water-level platform was difficult with Brooklyn in his arms, but Luke waved off Cooper's offer to help. He'd already had to put her in the other man's care once, and he wasn't letting go of her again. Luke had waited years to stake his claim with the little hellion, and he knew her well enough to realize it was going to take a full-court press to seal the deal.

Catalina stepped in front of Luke as he made his way through the opulent main cabin on his way to the Infirmary. Cat began fussing over her sister, but Luke deftly stepped around her as Cooper pulled the younger Adler aside. Hearing her profanity-laced protest made Luke wish, for a brief moment, he could stay and watch the fireworks. Catalina Adler and Cooper Hicks were a volatile mix of fire and fuel. Being in the room with them was like stepping into a dramatic stage production—except the only acting being done was the two of them denying their intense attraction.

Shaking off the impassioned energy in the cabin, Luke made his way down the narrow passageway to the small onboard infirmary. He had to give Austin Adler credit, the man could pull together a plan faster than Hannibal Smith on the old A-Team television series. The doctor stepped forward, nodding in greeting as he helped Luke settle Brooklyn on the examination table. They pulled up low rise side rails as they heard the engines roar to life and the boat lurched forward.

The doctor handed him a pair of scissors, directing him to cut her clothing from her body, but Brooklyn's low growl had him freezing with the scissors poised in mid-air.

"You cut this suit, and I swear I'll tell Paris you'll be her date for her sorority's Holiday Week Extravaganza." Luke felt the blood drain from his face. Paris Adler was the youngest of ten and as spoiled as she was beautiful. She was the epitome of a collegiate sorority girl and had harbored a crush on Luke since she was in junior high. When the doctor sighed in frustration and grabbed the scissors, Brooklyn turned her glacial ice blue stare on him. "You'll both go. Have you ever met my youngest sister, doctor? She's a steam-roller disguised as a college sorority queen."

"Steam-rolling seems to be a family trait." He shuddered and set the scissors aside. "Fine, if you don't want it cut off you can suffer through removing it—but don't say I didn't warn you." Turning his attention to Luke, the annoyed doctor added, "I'll leave the shears here in case she changes her mind. I can't imagine the pain will be worth whatever the damned catsuit cost, but it's her call."

The doctor may not have realized the challenge he's just issued, but Luke literally felt Brooklyn steel her resolve. Damn. She'd endure whatever pain she had to just to prove him wrong. *Damn it, the sleek suit is already ruined anyway, why is she kicking up such a fuss?* Sighing to himself, Luke helped her slide the pants down over her hips and tried to ignore the tiny black lace thong doing nothing to conceal her waxed mound. Brooklyn's barely audible hiss of pain as they slid the tight fabric over her wound made his heart clench.

Please take care of the amulet, don't let anyone else have it... and I mean no one. The thought had been as clear as if she'd spoken the words aloud, and Luke nodded his understanding and agreement. Pulling the small gold piece from the pocket of her pants, he slipped the velvet pouch into his own pocket. He was grateful the doctor had chosen that moment to turn his back as he set up a small tray with what Luke suspected was a variety of medical implements designed to torture unsuspecting patients. Smiling at Brooklyn when he noticed she'd covered the wound with her hand, he shook his head when she shrugged her shoulders, wincing at the pain.

"I'm sorry you have to do this, Luke. I know you don't like blood." His heart clenched at the realization she was more worried about him than she was herself.

"I dislike having another man see that black thong even more." He'd muttered his response, but the red flush staining her cheeks told him Brooklyn heard the confession. "Come on, let's get this over with. I suspect it's going to be more painful removing the top despite the fact the injury isn't as severe."

No shit. You have to be a damned contortionist to get into it. Luke coughed to cover his laughter. He loved her mental commentary, not only was it entertaining, but it also assured him she was going to be okay.

Chapter Five

W HEN LUKE CHUCKLED under his breath, Brooklyn tensed. She knew he'd heard her thoughts, and Luke felt the first stirrings of her frustration. From past experience, Luke knew she would try to block him, but she'd be wasting her time. Luke's Aunt Rissa had learned to block his Uncle Mitch for brief periods of time, but the mental energy required was so great, she rarely made the effort. Mitch's gifts were impressive, but Luke's were more so.

Connecting had never been Luke's problem, his challenge had always been finding ways to block the cacophony of voices surrounding him. Hell, connections were the easy part—NOT hearing the random thoughts of everyone he passed on the street was much more difficult.

As a child, Luke had suffered migraines because the noise in his head was often overwhelming. His high school counselor became convinced his abilities were real when he'd walked by her one morning and congratulated her on her pregnancy. She and her husband had been trying to have a child for years and had only found out late the night before she was expecting. Mrs. Carlson hadn't told anyone the news yet, so she'd known he wasn't repeating gossip.

From that point on, she'd worked hard to teach him various relaxation techniques to help alleviate the headaches. It had taken him most of his freshman year to master the meditations, but it had been his first successful experience blocking the din surrounding him every day.

The counselor had once asked him to describe what it was like. In turn, he'd asked her to meet him in the music room the next afternoon after school. He'd connected various radios and laptops to the large speakers of the room's booming sound system, moving them into a ten-foot diameter circle before asking her to stand in the center. Then he'd turned on the devices one by one, each playing something different but none of them overwhelming by itself. By the time he joined her at the center, she was already holding her hands over her ears, shaking her head.

He'd deliberately turned everything on in stages to give her a better idea how the din built up over the day. Walking down the hallway between classes was almost unbearable. With the press of a single button on the remote he held in the palm of his hand, Luke had silenced everything and flashed her a knowing smile.

"Is this what it's like for you all the time?" When he'd nodded, the woman had shaken her head. "I'm going to make some calls." She must have noted the concern etched in his expression because she began shaking her head. "Don't worry. I wouldn't dream of throwing you under the bus. The people at my university would make you a psych-lab rat in a matter of hours, and their cooking is the worst." She'd moved her hands to her hips in mock disgust. "I swear, they can't even boil water without setting off the sprinklers in their building." Her easy smile helped him relax, and for the first time he could remember, Luke had seen a teacher as a friend rather than as an adversary.

Pushing aside his wayward thoughts, Luke slid his hand inside the tight shirt to help Brooklyn push the fabric over her head. The tip of his middle finger brushed over her peaked nipple, making her gasp and sending so much blood to his groin, Luke wondered if his head would begin spinning from oxygen deprivation. Leaning down, so his lips brushed against the shell of her ear, Luke smiled when she shivered.

"Your body responds beautifully, B. I can't wait to explore all the ways my touch lights you up." She'd always resisted changing the dynamics of their relationship, and on one level, he understood her concern. As part of the larger picture, Luke didn't see it as a risk to their friendship, for him it was a natural progression—one he'd been looking forward to for a long time.

Easing the sleeve over the slice along the outside of her upper arm where the bullet grazed her, Luke frowned. This bullet had been aimed at her heart. He'd seen the red dot dancing over the center of her chest a split second before a second bullet lanced through her upper thigh. Brooklyn's stumble saved her life, and even though he knew she was going to be frustrated at the time it took to recover from the damage done to her leg, it was a damn sight better than the alternative.

Despite the cool air surrounding them, Brooklyn's skin was warming up nicely under his touch. Goosebumps raced over the surface, and Luke tried to remember the pads of his fingers were supposed to be focused on being clinical rather sensual. Lifting the damaged shirt over her head, Luke tried to shift his focus away from her cotton-candy pink nipples as they peaked from beneath the black lace of her bra. The temptation to free them from their racy confines was almost more than he could resist.

Meeting her gaze, Luke felt as if he was being magnetically pulled closer. The squeak of the small wheels on the doctor's cart pulled him back from the edge of desire so strong, he'd almost forgotten they weren't alone. Taking a deep breath, he tried to refocus on why they were there. Before the doctor had a chance to speak, Brooklyn grabbed his hand and gave him a reassuring squeeze.

"Go. I know how you feel about all things medical. I'm going to be fine, and I need to know the package is secure before Dr. Growly dopes me up." Luke struggled between his desire to stay close to her and his knowledge she wouldn't relax until she knew the amulet was safely stowed away.

"At the risk of not sounding like Dr. Congeniality, I'm going to say it would make my job a lot easier if I didn't have to work around you. No offense, but you take up a lot of space, and you're bleeding on the floor." Luke looked at the floor and sighed in frustration. Fucking hell, he hated the sight of blood.

BROOKLYN WAS CONVINCED she was losing her mind. She'd taunted the doctor who was going to be stitching her up and let Luke Grayson undress her. Oh yeah, she was two for fucking two as far as bonehead stunts went. Hell, that wasn't even counting nearly being killed by a security team that made the Keystone Cops look like special agents. *Damn.* Catalina was never going to let her live this down. Okay, make it three strikes... four if you count the nightmare she was going to face when Austin showed up.

As bossy older brothers went, Austin Adler wasn't usually up in her business, but when he was, he made up for lost time. Sighing to herself, Brooklyn leaned back against the pillows Dr. Grim used to prop her up and wondered why she hadn't listened to her instincts and retired. Mendoza might not be the biggest player she could have as an enemy, but he was a tenacious bastard, and he had plenty of resources to track her down. Brooklyn had known he was away from the estate and planned to pull off the heist, then be gone before he returned. She'd set up the perfect cover as a tourist, but that plan had been blown all to hell between one heartbeat and the next.

"It looks like the shoulder graze won't need any sutures. We'll use adhesive strips and wrap it up. With all the antibiotics you're going to get, you shouldn't have any trouble."

The doctor's words pulled her back to the moment, and she watched with detached interest as he pushed a syringe of painkiller into the IV line he'd already started. When he noted her interest, he smiled.

"If you've spent any time with your brilliant sister, I'm sure you realize this medication is one of the ones she worked so hard to get on the market. Let's hope all her effort pays off, shall we?" If her vision hadn't already been starting to blur, Brooklyn would have reached up and slapped the smug look off his damned face.

Wait! How did he know about London? Shit!

DR. EVAN MONROE saw the flair of fear ignite in Brooklyn's eyes and growled. *Hell, maybe she's right about the nickname. Shit!*

Evan had planned to send one of his assistants when he first received the call from Jace Garrett, but when he'd heard Brooklyn Adler's name, he'd quickly changed his mind. Evan was fascinated with London Adler's work, and after speaking with her briefly at a conference over a year ago, he'd become equally enamored with the woman herself. He'd been waiting for their paths to cross again, but so far, he hadn't had the pleasure.

Damn it all to fucking hell, it wasn't as if he was expecting to find London dressed in something intended to tempt a saint and waiting for him at Club Isola, but he'd assumed they'd see one another again eventually, either at a meeting or some other professional event.

And now I've terrified her big sister by not explaining how I knew London was her sister—just fucking great.

"She probably won't remember and if she does, trust me, she'll ask. The Adlers aren't known for being shy or easily intimidated."

Glancing to his right, Evan wasn't surprised to see Luke Grayson leaning casually against the doorframe. He should have known the man would sense Brooklyn's distress. From everything Evan had heard, the other man was even more connected to the world around him than his uncle Mitch. Luke had evidently heard at least part of what Evan had been thinking because he cocked a brow in question.

"I've met your uncle at various club events." Pointing to a package of gauze, Evan wasn't surprised when Luke understood the unspoken request and brought the package closer. "I've spoken with him at length about his gift." Taking the wrapped roll from Luke, Evan chuckled at his skeptical frown. "Don't look so surprised, just because I operate at the science end of the spectrum doesn't mean I don't appreciate and respect the other side." Luke nodded his understanding and stepped closer to take Brooklyn's hand.

"How is she? I know we'll be docking in a few minutes." Evan heard the question in his tone even if he hadn't actually asked.

"She's stable. There should be room in the helicopter for you if you want to ride along." *You may have to fight Catalina for the seat unless you enlist Cooper's help.*

"Cat won't be a problem, she's going to have her hands full answering calls from her family. She isn't going to want to answer their questions unless she knows she can't be overheard."

Evan shook his head and wondered how often Luke spooked people by responding to observations and questions they hadn't spoken aloud.

"It doesn't happen as often as it used to, I've learned to shut out people most of the time." Luke's easy smile made Evan chuckle.

"I'm not going to speculate about her leg because no matter what's happened inside, she's facing a significant amount of rehabilitation. Perhaps you can encourage her to take some time off. She's worn down, and that alone is going to add time to her recovery." Evan noted the gleam in Luke's eyes and wondered what he had up his sleeve, but as a physician, he'd learned a long time ago to stay out of his patient's personal lives. Unless a detail pertained to their health, it wasn't any of his business.

The telltale bump of the boat sliding up against the dock was their cue to finish securing Brooklyn to the gurney. Wheeling her down the narrow passageway and out onto the deck, Evan was relieved to see they were close enough to the aircraft, they could carry her if the blacktop was too rough. He didn't think they would do any additional damage to her leg, but he wasn't willing to take the chance—and he damned well didn't want to risk waking her. The medicine in the filled syringe in his pocket wouldn't be strong enough to keep her from suffering at least some degree of discomfort.

As they drew nearer to the helicopter, Evan was impressed by how clandestine the entire operation appeared. Several police cars blocked the entrance to the marina, but there were no lights, flashing or otherwise. He might not have seen them if not for the illumination provided by the flashes of lightning chasing across the sky. Jace had said they'd be *going dark*, but Evan hadn't realized his friend was speaking quite so literally. Sliding the gurney into the open door on the chopper, Evan felt a tug on his sleeve and looked over to see Luke grinning.

"I guess I forgot to mention, London is on her way. She might even beat us to your clinic."

Holy hell, the damned man had deliberately waited to share that particular piece of information until Evan had no opportunity to ask questions. If Luke's devilish grin was anything to go by, he knew exactly what he'd done. *Rat bastard!* As soon as the thought stormed through his mind, Grayson threw his head back and laughed.

Evan shook his head and chuckled. Hell, it had been years since he'd had anyone to laugh with. He'd worked like a maniac to get through medical school, then thrown himself into building a practice. Club Isola was his only outlet for social interaction, and he didn't usually waste his time hanging out in the bar with the other Doms. Shaking off his wayward thoughts, Evan pulled himself back into doctor mode.

Jace and Ian had entrusted Brooklyn into his care, and he didn't intend to let them down. Knowing he'd have an opportunity to interact with London Adler was a bonus, but it wasn't the primary goal. He wanted to get Brooklyn back on her feet as soon and as painlessly as possible. Luke also wanted to keep her safe, and Evan hoped the task wasn't going to prove itself a larger challenge than he'd originally anticipated.

Chapter Six

"**S**HE'S MY SISTER! You can't be serious about not giving me an update on her condition." London's voice was laced with disbelief, and even through the fog, Brooklyn recognized the tone. She could almost picture her younger sister standing with her hands on her hips, hair floating down to the top of her ass in a cascade of blonde curls. Despite her five-foot-nothing height, people often forgot how tiny London was because of her enormous attitude.

"Yes, I know you are her sister, but that doesn't automatically mean you are privy to her medical information." The man's voice sounded familiar, but the pain in her leg was making it impossible for Brooklyn to focus on anything else. The groan she thought had been in her head must have made its way to the surface because the couple arguing nearby were suddenly quiet. A warm hand wrapped itself around her cold one, and Brooklyn tried to open her eyes, but it was too much effort.

"Perhaps if the two of you could set aside the bickering for a few minutes, the doc could get our girl something for the pain."

Smiling to herself, Brooklyn wanted to cheer Luke's

intervention. Maybe the doctor would do something about the lightning sharp pain in her leg. *Damn it to dust bunnies, it hurts more now than it did before. Wait! How did London get on the boat?*

EMILIO MENDOZA WRAPPED his hand around the crystal sphere on his desk, waiting for its calming energy to work its magic, but his mood was too dark for the healing to make a dent in his fury. He barely managed to pull himself back from the edge of rage when he heard his mother's voice.

"Don't destroy my gift to you because you cannot control your temper, my son." He stilled, waiting for her to help him calm the waves of anger pounding in his brain. She had always been the only one who could push back the dark side he worked so hard to keep hidden from the outside world. The shadows that lurked in his mind were always waiting... always ready to wrap their long tentacles around him and pull him into the abyss.

As a child, his temper had been so out of control, he'd been kicked out of schools so often, his parents had finally given up and hired tutors. When the private teachers quit, one after another, his devoted parents attempted to teach him themselves but finally abandoned that plan as well. His success had come when he decided it was easier to read the books himself than to suffer the boredom and exhaustion accompanying work in the fields with the other migrant workers.

"I'm sorry, Mama. You are right. I'd never trade our

connection for the moment's pleasure I'd find venting my frustration." Taking several calming breaths, Emilio wondered if there would ever come a time when he'd be able to control the dark tide that was always floating at the edge of his very existence.

"The secret of the amulet is within your reach, but you must have it in your hand. The man you believe can help is the key." Most people believed the gold was the amulet's greatest gift, but Emilio knew better. It was the gift of healing, the ancients' knowledge of the inner workings of a troubled mind that drew him. "You know the thief was injured, follow that lead." Her words penetrated his distraction, pulling him back to the task before him.

Ian McGregor had been getting updates from someone last night at the same time the three fools who were supposed to be patrolling the perimeter bungled what should have been an easy grab. Jesus, Joseph, and sweet mother Mary, they let a burglar half their size slip through their fucking fingers. Even though the security cameras in the house had been scuttled by the intruder, he or she hadn't had time to tamper with those on the beach.

At first, he'd been convinced they were dealing with a very small man or possibly a teen, but after studying the film several times, he wasn't so sure. There was no question it had been a man helping the thief escape even though he'd been much more cognizant of the security cameras and studiously avoided exposing their faces to them. The boat that picked the pair up had been shrouded in darkness, all identifying information well covered. The only thing he'd been able to find out was a larger boat had off-loaded a patient they'd quickly loaded on a medivac chopper.

He would have to wait until morning to make the necessary calls about the helicopter's destination but having a plan of action was enough to calm his mind. The peace he only felt when he was in control of a situation moved over him, and Emilio took a deep breath. When he finally looked up, his mother was gone.

AUSTIN ADLER PACED the waiting room of The Monroe Clinic, wondering how in the hell his siblings managed to get themselves into these predicaments. From the look of things, his younger sister, Catalina and Cooper Hicks were still dancing around each other in the age-old ritual of denial he might have found amusing if he hadn't had to threatened to lock them out of the clinic if they didn't stop bickering. London was still going toe-to-toe with the Brooklyn's doctor in a wasted effort to get information about her condition.

Asia, the family legal eagle, had one shoulder propped against a nearby wall in a pseudo-casual pose he always likened to a mountain lion ready to pounce. As the corporate attorney for Adler Oil, Asia was the only other Adler sibling currently working full-time for the family business. Asia studied her nails, pretending nonchalance, but Austin knew her too well to be fooled. As the CEO of Adler Oil, Austin was technically Asia's boss—although he valued his genitals too much to utter the words out loud.

"She's wasting her time. As frustrating as it is, Dr. Monroe is right, and I'd have his ass in court before he could blink if he gave London the information she's demanding." Austin must have looked surprised because Asia flashed him one of her patented phony smiles before continuing. "Brooklyn hasn't signed anything giving us permission to receive the information."

"Are you talking about that damned HIPPA form Nurse Nazi makes me resign every year when I get a physical? Damn, that woman is anal about that thing, and I have no clue why. Nobody wants to hear about my latest prostate exam." He'd argued with the woman until he'd been ready to strangle her, but she'd been unrelenting.

"I shudder to think who might be interested in that particular detail, dear brother, but it's situations like this where having a signed form would be damned helpful. Of course, even if she'd given one to her personal physician, Dr. Monroe wouldn't have it, and we don't want him asking around for one since we're keeping her presence here a secret." She smiled and shook her head when he made an unpleasant sound of frustration.

Pushing off the wall, she walked closer to where he stood near the large picture window looking out over the perfectly manicured lawn as the last rays of sunlight disappeared over the horizon. They'd arrived at the clinic after Brooklyn was already in surgery, and the only information they'd gotten had come from Cooper and Catalina.

What his sister didn't know was her hug was as settling for him as he'd intended it to be for her. He'd been on edge since walking through the door. His senses were on high alert—not everyone in the clinic was who or what they appeared to be.

"Why don't you talk to Luke? He's the only reason those jokers didn't get a good shot. If he hadn't been there, she'd have died, and we'd have never known what happened to her."

For the first time since they'd arrived, Austin heard the underlying fear in Asia's voice. She was right, if Luke hadn't sounded the alarm, Brooklyn would have vanished, and they'd have never known the truth. Taking a deep breath, Asia looked up, meeting his gaze. Austin was stunned to see unshed tears glistening in her eyes—hell, he didn't think Asia had cried since she'd been old enough to cross her arms over her chest and demand her due.

Opening his arms, he was equal parts surprised and pleased when she didn't hesitate to step forward. When she was within reach, he pulled her into his embrace and kissed the top of her hair.

"She's going to be all right, you'll see. We'll get her someplace safe, then when the time is right, we'll help her find a new passion."

Austin already knew Brooklyn didn't need the damned money. Hell, he'd helped her set up accounts around the world. She was not only a hell of a retrieval expert, but his younger sister knew her own worth and had enough money socked away to fund a small country. Asia helped with some of the legalities, but he'd been the only one to see the financials, and he'd been shocked.

Releasing Asia when Luke Grayson stepped into the room, Austin was shocked by his appearance. The younger man looked like he'd been run over by a freight train, the dark half-moons under his eyes standing out as proof he probably hadn't slept much since he'd contacted Austin several days ago. When Asia and Catalina both rushed him, Grayson held up his hands and stepped back, obviously trying to avoid physical contact.

When Brooklyn and Luke first became friends, Austin spent a considerable amount of time and money investigating the man's purported "gifts." To say he'd been a skeptic would be a gross understatement, but everything he'd learned about Luke had pointed to his legitimacy. It hadn't been until they'd met face to face, he'd been truly convinced. Then it had taken a couple of years for Austin to become comfortable knowing Luke could easily tap into his thinking.

"You know it's harder for me to block you when I'm tired, so while I appreciate the little stroll down memory lane, I'd rather we just get to the point, so I can shower and sleep for a few hours." Austin nodded and muttered an apology before Luke gave them a quick update. "The graze on her arm is going to be fine—a little glue and tape were all it took to patch her up. Other than B's complaint the doc didn't use colored glitter-glue, *that* injury is a non-issue."

Austin fought a smile because he didn't doubt for a moment Brooklyn had uttered those exact words. He watched as Luke took a deep breath and seemed to be refocusing his attention on the subject at hand. Using his hand to motion Luke to the nearest chair, Austin wasn't surprised when he shook his head.

"If I sit down, I won't get back up, and I'm in desperate need of a shower." He shook his head again as if trying to clear out the fog of fatigue, and Austin hoped like hell he wasn't planning to drive anywhere. Luke Grayson was dead on his feet. "The clinic has a small studio apartment for families. I'm commandeering it for myself. I wouldn't dare drive anywhere, and I want to stay close. The greatest damage to Brooklyn's leg came from bone fragments rather than the bullet itself. Dr. Monroe has been amazing. I assure you, his reputation is well-earned."

Waiting patiently wasn't Austin's best trait, but he managed to hold out long enough for Luke to push his hand through his shaggy blonde hair. Remembering how much the other man hated blood, Austin suddenly realized how difficult the last twenty-four hours must have been for him. With his focus on Brooklyn, Luke wouldn't have been able to block the influx of negative energy, something Austin hadn't fully understood for several years after they met. Luke gave him a quick nod of acknowledgment before pulling in a deep breath.

"Her leg required several hours of surgery. She's sporting enough hardware to officially qualify as an Erector Set. Amazingly, her first concern was the fact she won't be able to slip quietly through TSA checkpoints." Luke shook his head and chuckled. "Guess we should be grateful she didn't fully grasp how much rehabilitation she's facing to regain full mobility. She won't have to wait long for the bone to heal since it's supported by steel, but she'll be spending a lot of time in the gym to recover the flexibility she's accustomed to." Catalina moved forward and reached out to him but caught herself before her fingers connected.

"Is she awake? Can we see her?" Cat's softly spoken words brought a crooked smile to Luke's face.

"She's awake and said to tell you she thinks you and Cooper should kiss and get it over with."

Catalina's face paled before flushing a brilliant shade of scarlet. To his credit, Cooper Hicks seemed unfazed, but the twitching of his lips gave away his amusement. Austin finally felt as if he could relax for the first time in days. He'd known for years how Luke felt about Brooklyn, and he'd respected the younger man's decision to wait until B was ready before claiming her as his own.

"Get some rest, Luke. We won't make any decisions without you." The relief Austin saw in Luke's eyes was unmistakable. "I'm sure you have some ideas about how to best protect her once she leaves here, we'll be looking forward to hearing them. For now, we'll watch over her and let the rest of the family know how things are going." As if on cue, a flash of red moved past the window, accompanied by the squealing of tires and three security SUVs quickly blocking in the red convertible.

"Cleveland's here." Catalina's amusement seemed lost on Luke who turned and moved slowly down the hall. Austin laughed to himself that Mr. Gifted obviously wasn't up to dealing with the family race car driver. One last look at Luke's retreating form had Austin laughing out loud when Grayson raised his hand, flipping him the bird.

Chapter Seven

I F BROOKLYN HAD to deal with one more of her siblings... pick one, it didn't matter... she wasn't going to be responsible for her actions. The absolute worst part of being injured was the gathering of the clan that always followed. She could deal with Austin, he might be bossy, but he always had her best interests at heart, and he knew how to keep his mouth shut. Asia was helpful, but it was easy to see she was anxious to get back to work. Brooklyn wasn't sure her eldest sister had any grasp of the concept of relaxation and had never taken a vacation as far as Brooklyn knew.

"After Cleveland wired up the clinic's security staff, he breezed in to check on you. Once he found out you were going to be fine, he was gone almost as quickly as he came." Catalina rolled her eyes as she recounted the family speed addict's ghost visit.

"Since I didn't expect him at all, I guess I should be grateful he was here although I wish I'd at least gotten a hug." It was something of a family joke since Cleveland Adler rarely stood still long enough for anyone to hug him. After their parents died, he'd flown into town less than an hour before the service and was gone again before most of the mourners had driven out of the cemetery. Brooklyn often wondered what drove him to be so restless. Since he rarely stood still long enough to chat, B didn't expect to know the answer anytime soon.

"Austin and Asia are leaving in a couple of hours, I think they're tying up some loose ends related to moving you." Brooklyn watched as Cat absently rubbed the hem of her shirt between her fingers. As far as Brooklyn knew, it was one of her sister's few *tells*. Since Austin had already been in to see her early this morning, Brooklyn already knew they were planning to leave.

"What about you, Cat? What's your exit strategy? If Mendoza's team managed to track me to shore, they'll have certainly found out about the chopper, and it wouldn't take a rocket scientist to find out where it landed. From there, it's a short jump to them knowing who is here, and that means you're the one they'll be watching. Everyone will expect me to leave with Austin, and when that doesn't happen, they'll focus on you." Since they both had apartments in New York City, it made sense for the two sisters to leave together if big brother hadn't whisked her home to Texas.

"Actually, you will be leaving with Austin or at least, everyone is going to assume it's you. Asia has already gone to the airport to make sure everything is in place for *your* speedy entrance onto the jet. And we both know she'll kick up enough of a fuss, everyone in the airport will know you are flying home with big brother and pushy sister."

Brooklyn's head was starting to swim as she worked to sort through the details of a plan she hadn't helped put together. The medicine they'd given her a few minutes earlier was beginning to take effect, and for the first time since she'd come out of surgery, she wasn't pleased with the quick slide into oblivion. Her eyelids were too heavy to hold up any longer, and she was rapidly losing the battle to stay connected with what was happening around her. *Damn it, Paris... no... Asia. No... that's not right either.*

"London. She's the one who developed the wonder drug carrying you away, baby. Let go, I've got you." Luke's whispered words moved through her mind like a calming mist as his warm breath caressed the shell of her ear. Brooklyn let go of her tenuous hold on reality and let herself tumble back into the darkness. The freefall was sublime, and she was grateful for the reprieve from the pain and confusion.

"WHAT THE EVER-LOVING hell?" Three vehicles left the Monroe Clinic within a half hour, and all three had a woman on a gurney. The fuckers were playing with him, and Emilio Mendoza was not fucking amused. Playing the odds, he followed the second van to a small airstrip. By the time he talked his way past the elderly guard at the gate, there was no one around. The van sat empty, sheets piled atop the gurney, and he watched from the side of the runway as a small plane lifted off. He still didn't know for certain who the thief was—although his money was on Brooklyn Adler. What he did know was the odds of him following the correct vehicle weren't stellar.

Phoning his security team, he told them to begin checking other flights leaving the area. He wanted to know who owned the planes and where they were headed. He hadn't even made it back to the gate when his phone buzzed in his pocket. Answering before the second ring, he gave the guard a pleasant wave, then focused on the information his second in command was relaying. Two private planes had departed from local airports during the past half hour. The one owned by Adler Oil had filed a flight plan to Houston, McGregor Holdings was listed as the owner of record for the second plane. Ian McGregor's jet had filed a flight plan early this morning for a round trip to Washington, D.C.

Pocketing his phone, Emilio smiled to himself. There was no need to rush to D.C. since he knew exactly where the thief was headed. Learning one of the planes belonged to Adler Oil had been a real stroke of luck because it confirmed his suspicion. Brooklyn Adler's reputation as a retrieval specialist was well known. This time, she hadn't made a clean get-away. Now he could bide his time and follow-up with Ian McGregor in a day or two. It would give Ms. Adler and those who were helping her an opportunity to develop a false sense of security, and the extra time would also give him a chance to come up with a plausible reason to request a meeting with the elusive Ian McGregor.

Once he was back on McGregor's island, he'd be able to retrieve what belonged to him and deal the woman who'd thought she could waltz into his home and take something he'd waited years to obtain. Emilio planned to bring the burglar back to his home and make an example of her. Seeing her tortured and killed would discourage anyone else from making the same mistake.

Emilio drove back to the marina where he kept his boat, thinking about how much he looked forward to brainstorming with his mother—she had always been diabolical when it came to punishments. She'd given him all sorts of wonderful ideas about how to deal with those she felt were beneath him when he was in boarding school after her fall from the balcony. And her suggestions had been even more creative during all the times he was hospitalized as a teen. Thinking about her fall and how dramatically his life had changed after he'd finally convinced everyone she'd tumbled over on her own always gave him a migraine. Rubbing the back of his neck as he parked the sports car close to the wooden walkway leading to his boat, Emilio tried to hold the pain back until he could take his medication and sleep.

LUKE LOOKED OVER at Brooklyn, shaking his head. He was as amused as he was concerned she'd slept through being moved in and out of two different vans before being driven to Logan International in Boston. The air ambulance her brother had chartered had flown them to Miami where they'd refueled before heading to Belize.

In a few minutes, they'd be on their way to the marina, and she needed to be awake for the final leg of their journey to St. George's Caye Resort. Just eight miles from Belize City, it was the perfect place for Brooklyn to lie low and rest. The boardwalk giving access to the over-water bungalows was wide enough to accommodate the small cart she would need for transportation and was smooth enough for her to navigate later with crutches.

The resort's romantic ambiance meant there wouldn't be as much interaction between guests, and since they didn't allow anyone under fifteen years of age, there wouldn't be any of the usual noisy chaos found in most tropical resorts.

Catalina and Cooper were in the third decoy vehicle and had flown to Club Isola in one of Ian's private jets. The rumor among treasure hunters was the amulet had a secret compartment so it would be easy for Mendoza to believe the thief was seeking Ian's help in unlocking the artifact's secrets. Since Brooklyn had retrieved the beautiful Egyptian piece well in advance of the insurance company's deadline, the CEO and Board of Directors were willing to wait for it to be returned, giving Ian a chance to work with the remarkable piece of craftsmanship.

"Come on, baby, time to wake up and enjoy the scenery. We'll be on St. George's Caye soon, and you don't want to miss a thing." The entire island had been designated a historic landmark, and the citizens took tremendous pride in preserving the architectural integrity of the buildings. Luke had vacationed here several times with friends although he had to admit the rowdy group hadn't done much to ensure the tranquil atmosphere of the resort where they'd stayed. Hell, they'd deserved being asked to move their revelry to a more suitable location—on another caye.

"I'm not sure what that loopy smile is about, but I'd be willing to bet there is a story there somewhere." Brooklyn's sleepy voice brought him back to the moment, and he grinned.

"You'd be right, but I think I already told you about my snorkeling trip a couple of years ago with a couple of college buddies. I hope the manager of the resort has a short memory or bad eyesight." He was pleased to see her smile at his lame attempt at humor. He'd be much more at ease once they had Brooklyn safely in their bungalow.

"We'll be landing soon. Before we make our way to the marina, we're going to see what we can do about making you look a bit different." When she raised a skeptical brow, Luke leaned his head back and laughed. "Okay, perhaps I should have said, we're going to have various items available for you to change your appearance. Work your magic, oh Mystical Mistress of Disguise." He raised one end of the gurney, so she was reclining rather than flat on her back. She needed to get used to being upright for the transfer to a wheelchair.

"Did Dr. Growly and London ever stop arguing long enough to notice the wildfire of attraction between them?" Her question surprised him, and she must have noticed his reaction. "What? Just because you all kept me drugged didn't mean I couldn't hear what was going on around me. Cripes, those two are worse than Cat and Cooper." Luke wasn't convinced the doctor and Brainiac chemist were worse, he was still reserving judgment. In his humble opinion, the race was too close to call.

He'd been shocked how small the incision was on Brooklyn's upper thigh, it was easy to see why Evan Monroe was a favorite among the rich and famous. The scar from the bullet graze on the outside of her shoulder was going to be larger than the one from the doc's work to put her leg back together. They had a suitcase full of supplies, many of them newly developed by Ian McGregor's merry band of diabolical geniuses. Luke was looking forward to working with Ian and his Uncle Mitch, both were imaginative beyond belief—not only did they think outside the box, but he doubted they knew there *was* a box.

"It seems like a waste to be in such an amazing place and not be able to enjoy the water sports. I didn't even get to pack a swimming suit… or anything else for that matter. Damn, please tell me that my sisters went shopping for me."

"Yes, they did, and one of the team assigned to you has been hitting the local shops, raving about how her friend is supposed to be arriving today after being thrown under a bus." When her mouth dropped open, he grinned. "You're in for a treat, Jen McCall's humor is in a class all its own." *Thank God lightning doesn't strike for understatements.*

They landed and taxied directly into a private hanger. Once the large doors closed behind them, the lights came on and watching out the small windows, Luke noticed people seemed to be materializing from nowhere. Brooklyn wasn't happy they insisted on unloading her on the gurney, but no one wanted to take a chance with the wheelchair or crutches since she was still battling back the brain fog from being so heavily sedated.

"Frack, this is going to get old in a big damned hurry." Her muttered complaint was quickly pushed aside by gasps of pain when she tried to move from the gurney to the wheelchair without waiting for help.

"Don't do that again, or I'm going to begin a tally," Luke whispered the warning against her ear and smiled to himself when he heard her suck in a quick breath. She knew he was a sexual Dominant—it had always been a sticking point between them, but he knew something she didn't want to admit, even to herself. Brooklyn Adler had a submissive streak a mile wide. Her mind was typically spinning at warp speed, and there was a very large part of her soul that was exhausted by the effort to keep up with the flurry of continual activity in her mind. He knew submission would offer her a reprieve, and proving he was right was going to be a pleasure unlike any other.

Luke remembered how shocked London had been by Brooklyn's reaction to the medication. Her state of physical and emotional exhaustion before being injured played a significant part in her response, and he hoped a few days of warm sunshine and the hypnotic sounds of the ocean would be just what the doctor ordered. Pressing his lips against her forehead, Luke frowned when he realized she was beginning to perspire in the large air-conditioned space.

"Don't try to do too much, or you'll be down for the count, baby. Proper rehabilitation requires knowing when to push and when to back off."

"Let me guess, you'll be guiding me through this quest, oh wise one?" It was the first time he'd seen her eyes sparkle since they'd flared with surprise, just before she collapsed into his arms at the Mendoza estate.

"You can bet your pretty, little—soon to be a delicious shade of scarlet—ass on it." He trailed the tips of his fingers down the side of her face before settling them over her pulse point. "Now, get busy, I want to be at the resort before nightfall. We'll have a cart, but I don't want to risk you becoming disoriented as we move over the water." He heard the echoes of doubt in her mind but ignored them. There would be time for discussions later, right now, he needed her disguised and on the road.

Moving Brooklyn in front of the lighted mirror, he watched in appreciation as she looked over the supplies and grinned. If he hadn't been watching, he'd have never believed the woman looking at him in the mirror twenty minutes later was the same one he'd been friends with for more than a decade. Hell, she'd even assumed an accent in her silent self-talk.

"Want to tell me about Clarice, sweetheart?" He saw her eyes widen in surprise that he'd identified the name she assigned to her alter ego. He grinned and shook his head. "I have to admit, watching you transform yourself was nothing short of astounding, but hearing the change in your internal dialogue was something I never expected. Damned impressive, B." The impish grin she flashed him would be impossible to disguise—it was all Brooklyn.

Chapter Eight

L UKE KNEW HOW difficult the boat ride had been for
Brooklyn. He hadn't been surprised by her resistance
to taking anything for the pain until they'd docked at the
resort, her reluctance to put herself fully in the hands of a
team she didn't know understandable. Brooklyn was
usually damned good at taking care of herself, so it wasn't a
surprise to anyone when she'd been adamant about
waiting to take the pain medication he'd offered her. He
could hear the echoes of pain in her mind but understood
why she wanted to be alert to her surroundings as they
made their way to the bungalow.

"We're very close to our destination, so I want you to
take this now—let's give it a head start. Our meal has
already been delivered and a perimeter sweep done of the
area." He felt the questions floating through her mind, but
they faded quickly under the weight of fatigue and pain.
"This is a much smaller dose than you were given earlier.
You won't heal as quickly if you're in pain." She nodded
and swallowed the capsule without reaching for the bottle
of water he held out to her. "Damn it, Brooklyn. Drink the
water, we have ginger ale in the bungalow."

They'd had this same argument during college. She'd

had pneumonia their sophomore year, and he'd slept on the floor by her bed because he'd been so worried about her. Brooklyn hated taking the medications she'd been prescribed and stubbornly refused to take them unless he sweetened the deal with her favorite soda.

Luke knew the team hadn't wanted to call all around the island looking for her favorite beverage, so the McCalls had stocked up before leaving Texas. Knowing Jen, it was a good thing they hadn't flown commercial.

Driving slowly down the wide wooden pathway, he could feel the shift in temperature as soon as they were over the water. Since the cart was electric, the silence let them hear the lapping of the waves against the shore. The soothing sound was part of the reason he'd wanted to return here, the rhythmic beat of waves lapping steadily against the shore soothed his soul, and he hoped it would do the same for Brooklyn.

Luke was relieved to see the resort's manager was new. The enthusiastic man didn't appear to have been briefed by the bellman who'd instantly recognized Luke. Laughing to himself, Luke wondered how much of the man's coopera-tion was due to the phone calls he'd received from Austin Adler, Ian McGregor, and Kyle West? They could all be damned intimidating, and Luke didn't want to consider what the trio would be like when working together. There was also the distinct possibility Sam McCall delivered a case of the elderly man's favorite whiskey. The single bottle Luke and his friends had used to bribe him had only gained them a small measure of grace.

They'd been lucky to secure three bungalows in a row—Luke and Brooklyn would take the one in the middle while the McCalls occupied the one closer to shore. Catalina and Cooper would utilize the one on the opposite side when they arrived early tomorrow morning. The McCalls arrival two days earlier was part of their cover. They'd already done numerous security sweeps before giving Luke the all clear.

As Luke and Brooklyn passed the McCalls' bungalow, Sam stepped out of the shadows to greet them.

"Good evening. Looks like we'll be neighbors. I'm Sam McCall." He held out his hand to Brooklyn. Luke smiled warmly when Sam greeted him as well. To anyone watching from shore, it would look like they were meeting for the first time. "My wife is inside, you'll meet her tomorrow—if we can keep her contained that long. My brother, Sage, is hanging out at the cantina back at the resort. He's connected with a few of the locals, so we'll hear if anyone starts asking too many questions."

Brooklyn had already been briefed about the McCalls polyamorous marriage, so she hadn't blinked at the mention of his brother. Luke knew she was going to be surprised when she met Jen and Sage. He'd always been amazed at the significant difference in the dynamics between Sam and Jen as opposed to those between Sage and Jen. The former diplomat was one of the few people Luke had trouble reading—not because she intentionally blocked him, but her mind was such a cacophony of information spinning around like a damned Texas tornado, it was almost impossible to keep up. It was easy to see why Jen treasured the peace she found in submission even if the little hellion did give the McCall brothers a run for their money every chance she got.

"Jen has her heart set on conning one of the locals into letting her borrow their helicopter to do some air-recon. If we let her go alone, she'll end up owning the damned airport so she and Sage will be making an early morning trip. We'll "bump into you" for an accidental meeting at lunch." Sam tried his best to look annoyed by the delay, but his deep love and respect for his wife still managed to shine through. When she didn't take the bait, he shook his head and continued.

"I was hoping she'd see this as a chance to take it down a notch or two since there are going to be five of us watching your backs. Hell, we haven't had a vacation since Suzie was born, and she's already in pre-school." Luke wanted to laugh out loud when Sam looked at Brooklyn hopefully.

"You think I can influence a woman I've never met to kick back? Not knowing when to take a break is how I ended up with a slice-and-dice mark across my shoulder and enough hardware in my upper thigh to light up the most antiquated TSA checkpoints." Turning her attention to him, she shook her head. "This guy has had all his shots, right? Or maybe he missed the briefing where they explained my complete and utter disdain for *downtime*?"

Sam leaned his head back, his laughter filling the late evening quiet, but it was Jen's voice from the front of their bungalow that caught their attention.

"I like her already." Jen McCall stepped from their bungalow and smiled at her husband. "She's going to fit in perfectly. Did Tobi tell you we're starting a new group? We're working on a logo and getting leather jackets with S & M stitched on the back. Smart and Mouthy. Can't you just see it?" Looking at Brooklyn, Jen's smile lit up the fast encroaching darkness. "We'll send your size information to her, so you can be a Charter Member. Maybe I should wait until morning so we can talk to Catalina—any woman who can tie Cooper Hicks up in knots needs to be included as well."

Luke wanted to laugh out loud at Brooklyn's expression. For the first time in years, the confusion he could hear in her mind was playing out on her face. The crack in Brooklyn's veneer was a testament to how leveled she'd been by pain and exhaustion. As much as he was enjoying the conversation with Sam and Jen, it was time to get his sweet woman settled. Luke felt Sage's more light-hearted energy a few seconds before the younger McCall snaked his tan arm around his wife's waist and pulled her back against his chest.

"Are you stirring up trouble, Sweet Cheeks? Maybe Sam and I need to find a way to distract you. I'd be willing to bet our fellow Dom can do the same with his exhausted sub as well."

If Luke hadn't had his hand on Brooklyn's shoulder, he might have missed how her muscles tensed, but he wouldn't have missed the way she deliberately blanked her mind. This was the skill he knew he would have to fight, but he was ready.

BROOKLYN APPRECIATED SAM McCall's transparency. You only needed to be in his presence for a few seconds to understand the strength of his Dominance. His brother was every bit as steely, but his was cloaked in charm meant to disarm and distract. In Brooklyn's opinion, he was the more dangerous of the two. Sage McCall was the one she'd be the most cautious around.

Sam tilted his head ever so slightly to the side as a ghost of a smile whispered through his expression. "Brother, I do believe Brooklyn just read you like a kindergarten primer." Jen laughed aloud, and Sage grinned like a kid caught with his hand in the cookie jar. The effect made her feel as if she'd just passed some sort of test.

"I told you I like her. She's too smart to not figure the two of you out." Jen met Brooklyn's gaze, and B noted the glint of admiration she saw there. "We're going to get along great, Brooklyn. We'll keep you safe until Ian and Mitch unravel the secrets of the amulet." Sage stepped around Jen to kneel in front of Brooklyn.

"I'm not going to sugar coat it, Brooklyn—the reports coming in on Mendoza aren't good. We're calling in every favor we can to crack the seals on Emilio Mendoza's records."

Brooklyn wasn't naïve, she recognized when she was being coddled... and it pissed her off. Luke must have sensed her frustration because she felt the warmth of his hand as he rubbed a small circle between her shoulder blades.

"Sage isn't holding back, B. We don't have all the information about Mendoza, at least not yet—but there are some big red flags. Nobody on the team is willing to take unnecessary chances—your safety is too important. As a result, we're going to look like paranoid bastards because we plan to be hyper-vigilant until we know the answers."

Luke's voice was reassuring, and since she was fading fast, his vague explanation was going to have to be enough for now.

In the distance, Brooklyn heard Jen mutter something about not appreciating being called a paranoid bastard before adding they'd bring breakfast by before they left. In the very back of her mind, Brooklyn was grateful it didn't sound as though the other woman expected a response.

When darkness suddenly surrounded her, Brooklyn suspected it was because her eyelids had gotten too heavy to hold up rather than nightfall. The next thought she had was how wonderful it felt to be in Luke's arms again. She'd always been afraid to let herself explore what was between them, but she didn't want to run any longer.

"You're right, baby. No more running." The words were so softly spoken, she wasn't sure if they'd really been spoken aloud or if she'd dreamed them.

MITCH GRAYSON STARED at the man speaking from the large monitor in front of him and wondered how something that should have been so simple had gotten so insanely complicated.

"So, you're telling me the guy was kicked out of both public and private schools, but no one will say why?"

"They clam up tight. It's like they're terrified of the man. The only person who made even the smallest slip was a woman who worked as a secretary at one of the private schools. She's been retired for years but remembered Emilio Mendoza vividly. I sent a man to interview her at the nursing facility where she lives. He told me she'd acted afraid to say anything, and when he asked her why she'd told him to ask Emilio's mother." Micah Drake was one of the best computer hackers in the world, so Mitch was expecting the other man to know Mendoza's mother's location down to a gnat's ass.

"Are we sending someone to check with the mother?"

"She died the day her son turned sixteen. The official report cites suicide, but there are a couple of interesting handwritten notes in the margin of the official report. I'm guessing one of the investigators didn't agree with the conclusion and scribbled in the file before it was sealed and buried in the basement of the local police department."

Mitch saw the corners of Micah's mouth twitch, but he didn't want to ruin his friend's big reveal, so he waited in silence for him to continue.

"The county recently completed a five-year program of microfilming all their old files, so they could free up space in the basement for a training center. Fortunately for me, they spent all their money on scanning and archival equipment rather than security."

"Okay, I'll bite. What did this interesting note say?" *Fucking hell, when did Drake get to be such a damned Drama Queen?*

"The lead investigator thought the son pushed his mom off the balcony."

"Do you have a name? Let's talk to the investigator and find out why they didn't follow up on that angle?" Mitch was starting to wonder what the hell his nephew had gotten himself into, but until he had more information, it was going to be damned hard to convince Luke to back away from the woman he'd wanted for the better part of a decade.

"No can do. Evidently, the guy got pissant drunk at a local bar a year ago and started talking about Maria Mendoza's death. A few days later, his car went over a rocky ledge along a winding coastal road. No one understood why he was driving so fast until a mechanic noted the car's brake line looked like it had been cut." Mitch's skin crawled, and he was sure his heart skipped several beats.

"I'm going to check in with Ian again." Mitch let his mind circle back to the conversation they'd had about the amulet. "Shit, I'm sure he told me Mendoza mentioned his mother being anxious to find a way to open a piece of jewelry. It didn't sound like he was speaking in the past tense, but I want to verify that with Ian before we start looking deep into Menendez's medical records."

"Make sure you use a secure line. I'm not sure what we're dealing with here, but I'd rather err on the side of the angels if you know what I mean."

Mitch knew exactly what Micah meant and couldn't have agreed more. Nothing about this situation was adding up, and everything he learned made things appear increasingly convoluted.

"Agreed. In the meantime, get a message to the McCalls and Cooper Hicks. Let's not alarm Cat yet. I don't want her pulling Brooklyn out. She's safer on our watch." What Mitch didn't want to mention was how pissed his nephew would be if Cat slipped Brooklyn out from under his nose.

Luke had been waiting forever for the little cat burglar,

and anyone attempting to stand in his way would find out what hell on earth was all about. Mitch wasn't the only gifted computer tech in the family. Luke could make someone's life a living nightmare with a few keystrokes. Since he was still working as an independent contractor, Luke enjoyed a lot more latitude—which was pure PCBS. Yes, indeed. Politically correct bull shit was damned accurate if he was going to label Luke's darker talents as latitude. Most people didn't know Luke had a very lucrative sideline doing contract technology hits.

Wreaking havoc in a political opponent's or enemy's life was one of the most effective ways Mitch knew to distract them—he'd seen it used time and time again. Mitch didn't know how much money Luke had squirreled away in offshore accounts, but he suspected his nephew could easily buy the island he was currently enjoying.

Luke had bought homes in every city where he'd worked for more than a few weeks. His explanation had been simple… he didn't like renting. Luke hired couples to live in each home, so the residences were always maintained and ready if a friend or member of the family wanted to use it. When Mitch first heard about Luke's personal interest in Brooklyn, he'd been worried the young man was going to end up heartbroken. After meeting her, Mitch's reservations had evaporated.

Brooklyn reminded Mitch of the woman who owned his own heart. It wasn't their appearance but the similarities in their spirits. Mitch had marveled at the parallels in the vibration of the two women's energy and understood on a soul-deep level Luke's attraction to Brooklyn.

As he and Micah ended their call, Mitch sent up a silent

prayer they could keep Brooklyn safe from a man he feared was far more dangerous than any of them had originally believed.

Chapter Nine

BROOKLYN CAME AWAKE in stages, a completely foreign concept... and damned unnerving as well. She was usually fully functional before her feet hit the floor, so she disliked feeling disconnected. Before the last vestiges of sleep cleared from her mind, she became aware of several things at the same time. First, she no longer wore the t-shirt and yoga pants she'd been wearing when they'd finally gotten off the damned plane.

If she didn't fly again for a month of Sundays, it would suit her just fine. Flying had been fun when she'd first started retrieving, but over the years, it had become more and more challenging, to the point she was ready to retire simply to stay out of airports.

Refocusing her attention on the present, Brooklyn searched her drug-cluttered memory latching onto what looked like an old-time movie someone had done a lousy job of splicing together—flashes of different moments from a scene, all related, but not necessarily appearing in order. When she remembered Luke's hands skimming over her bare skin as he gently removed her clothes, Brooklyn felt her body respond at the memory. His touch had been gentle, but he'd lingered long enough for her to feel the heat of sexual desire lurking beneath what was supposed to be clinical.

Her head was beginning to hurt from trying to figure out what it meant and what she was going to do about it. Brooklyn tried to push the questions out of her mind as she struggled to sit up. She'd intended to throw her legs over the edge of the bed, but dual white-hot flashes of pain in her arm and leg made her vision blur as she cried out.

"Fuck a fat fairy, that hurts." She was fighting a losing battle to shrug on an oversized shirt Luke had left on the end of the bed for her when he spoke behind her.

"Why didn't you ask for help, B?" Then muttering under his breath, he added, "I should have tied you to the damned bed." This time the flash of heat was in a much different part of her body, and the worst of the pain she felt now was from unfulfilled need. Between one heartbeat and the next, Brooklyn wondered if the beads of sweat suddenly dotting her forehead were from her body's reaction to the pain in her thigh and shoulder or if they were, perhaps a symptom of the much deeper ache she'd felt for months. She'd denied her desire for Luke Grayson for so long, Brooklyn was scared to finally put her heart and body on the line.

What if he's disappointed? He's waited so long, it's bound to be anticlimactic. I'll end up like a birthday gift you knew you were getting... a pretty toy that's so much more attractive before it's actually yours. A glittering bauble he's craved for so long, he doesn't yet realize he's outgrown it. Damn it, why didn't I hire someone to look after me and just disappear? What was I thinking getting Luke and his friends involved in this mess? What if one of them gets hurt? Fuck me, this is a train wreck.

LUKE WASN'T SURE whether he should coddle her with tender reassurances or paddle her ass for letting so much nonsense take up space in her head. Damn, the woman was frustrating as hell.

"Shut that down, right now." He was sure she hadn't heard him step into the open doorway of the bungalow's only bedroom, and her quick intake of breath confirmed it. "All the insecurity and worry are wasted energy. It won't get you where you want to go, B."

"Didn't your mother teach you it's rude to eavesdrop?" Luke raised a brow at her snarky attitude. Maybe he should have given her another round of pain medication when he first got up. "Where are the crutches I'm supposed to start using?" She made a point to look around the room... twice.

He wasn't surprised she was unsettled by the changing boundaries of their relationship, he hadn't expected the path to be smooth. Now the situation was further complicated by her injuries, her dependence on others, and everyone's concerns about her safety.

"You're not ready for crutches yet, baby. We'll be able to use a wheelchair outside the bungalow, but this space is simply not large enough for it to be practical inside." Watching her worry her bottom lip as she sorted through his words was a test of his patience. He gave her a few seconds to process her options before continuing. "Until you are off pain meds, I'll be helping you get around the bungalow. I want to make this perfectly clear, there will be no hopping—this is not negotiable, Brooklyn."

"I need to use the bathroom. How am I supposed to get there?" He recognized the challenge in her eyes and smiled to himself—now that she'd thrown down the gauntlet, he would be happy to pick it up. Without hesitating, Luke closed the space between them in no time, his long legs eating up the distance in only a few strides. He didn't ask permission before scooping her up into his arms—he'd learned a long time ago it was unwise to ask any of the Adler siblings a question you didn't want answered with brutal honesty. Her squeak of surprise made him chuckle.

Sam and Sage had installed several temporary grab-bars for Brooklyn's safety, and Luke appreciated their effort. No doubt they'd brought them from Texas, and once again, Luke was grateful the trio hadn't been forced to fly commercial. Sitting her on the toilet, he laughed out loud at the deep red blush highlighting her cheeks.

"Out. I'll never be able to go with you watching. Geez. Give a girl some privacy why don't you?" *Cripes, our brothers were never allowed in our bathroom.*

"Baby, I'm not your brother, and you can stop playing the friend card as well. Things have changed, and the sooner you get on board with the shift, the more we'll both enjoy it." He leaned close, tucking a thick strand of hair behind her ear before trailing the pads of his fingers down the side of her slender neck. "I'll be on the other side of the door. Call me as soon as you're finished, and I'll help you wrap your injuries so you can take a shower." The McCalls had made a few modifications to the interior, including a bamboo seat, but he'd need to help her get in and out of the space.

He was relieved to see her quick nod. Brooklyn might be fiercely independent, but she was also whip-smart and driven, so she wouldn't take unnecessary risks with her recovery. Since the good doctor hadn't been given time to fully explain the scope of the physical therapy Brooklyn was going to require, they'd scheduled a conference call for later this morning. By the time she let him know she was ready for him to return, Luke was relieved to see she appeared more settled.

"Don't forget, you're supposed to talk to Dr. Monroe this morning, and you aren't getting any coffee until you're dressed, so I suggest you don't take a nap in the shower." He chuckled when she flipped him the bird. Luke leaned his head back and laughed because it was obvious she remembered all the times he'd found her asleep in the shower while they were at MIT. "Now that I think about it, your track record for taking care of yourself isn't great, maybe I should stay and help you." He sat her on the small bench, handed her a basket of shower supplies and the hand-held showerhead.

"You have seven minutes, B, and not a second longer. Now, hand over the shirt, baby." It didn't matter that Luke was standing almost arm's length away, the blast of heat he felt surging through the beautiful woman in front of him was staggering. She would soon learn to crave the dominance her mind was still resisting. Her body was already with him, but it was going to take a while to bring her head on board.

Chapter Ten

B ROOKLYN STARED AT the screen in disbelief. "You want me to be off my leg for how long? I thought you put it back together with enough steel to build a small skyscraper?"

"It isn't the hardware that's the problem, Brooklyn. The damage to the bone isn't the only issue we're dealing with, there was also significant trauma to the soft tissue surrounding it. Those things take time to heal, and you are no condition to begin rehab. Damn it, I'd hospitalize most patients with your level of exhaustion."

She recognized the glare he gave her and sighed. *I hope London knows what she's getting in to. I swear, Doms are taking over the damned world. I've got to find a more laid-back crowd.*

Luke was standing to the side and would have been out of camera range for the good doctor, but Brooklyn doubted the man currently filling the small screen had missed Luke's snort of laughter.

"Not happening B. I told you—everything has changed."

She didn't doubt for a minute, he planned to push his weight around, and from the size of Sam and Sage McCall, she was guessing the three of them together were equal to a small truck. *Damn, I'm turning into Bronx.*

Bronx Adler's tremendous success in auto sales was only eclipsed by his passion for the perks of that overwhelming success. Her brother knew more about the latest trends than most social media addicts. Bronx had always had an affinity for sales, their parents had always sworn he could sell snow cones to Eskimos. Bronx's annual wardrobe budget was more than most people paid for their first home, and his lavish vacations were the envy of his peers.

The only one of the Adler siblings who traveled more often was Kensington whose successful career in action movies took him to the most exotic locations on the planet. Oddly enough, Kensington seemed less impressed with his success than any of his brothers or sisters. Letting her mind leap aimlessly from one topic to the next as the lapping waves against the pillars of the bungalow started working their relaxing magic, Brooklyn reconsidered her earlier assessment. Cat probably traveled more than all of them put together.

Making a mental note to check in with her younger sister to see how she was holding up, Brooklyn wondered how Catalina coped with what even the staunch workaholic would call a brutal schedule… and she'd been on this breakneck pace for two years.

"B, come back to us, baby."

Brooklyn was startled when Luke's voice finally registered in her muddled brain. Blinking the room back into focus, Dr. Stick-up-his-ass had his arms crossed over his chest as he frowned at her. Taking a deep breath, Brooklyn let it out slowly.

"Okay, I'll admit, I'm tired. The last month or so has

been crazy. Do you all get nuts like this when a man is tired?" The doctor reared back as if she'd slapped him, and she probably should have felt some measure of guilt for the snarky response, but she really didn't have the energy. She'd seen her male siblings praised for their ambitious work ethic, but the sisters had been cautioned about overextending themselves, and she'd never understood the difference.

"Baby, I want you to explain your concern to Dr. Monroe. I heard it loud and clear, but he didn't. He needs to understand where the question came from in order to address it." Luke's voice was gentle but firm enough to let her know it hadn't been a *suggestion*.

She nodded and began explaining some of the dynamics of her enormous family to the doctor who had assumed a tremendous risk when he'd agreed to help her. When she'd finished, Brooklyn leaned back in her chair, feeling as if she'd been awake forever rather than an hour.

"I'm sorry, I didn't mean to be rude. You're right, I've pushed myself to the very edge. I'm grateful for all you've done. You've put yourself in danger to help me, and I'd like to caution you to be particularly vigilant until this is resolved. Mendoza is a crazy mother." Luke cleared his throat, and she sighed before continuing. "Word on the street is the guy has delusions. To be honest, I was surprised how easy his place was to get into, it's almost like he didn't think anyone would dare steal from him." Or maybe the rumors she'd heard in the nearby town were true, and the man really did believe there were other people living in the house.

Luke raised a brow at her in question but didn't comment as they wound up their conversation with the doctor and signed off. Brooklyn leaned her head back against the chair and closed her eyes as exhaustion slammed into her with the strength of a tsunami.

"I'm sorry, Luke. I can barely wrap my head around how big a mess I've created… and all because I didn't want to admit I was too tired to pull off one last job." Opening her eyes, she wasn't surprised to see him squatted down beside her chair. His indulgent smile was all it took to tip the scales of her emotions, and she felt the burn of tears as they filled her eyes.

"Baby, please don't cry. I'd have gone to the ends of the earth to bring you home safely. Your soul was calling out for help even when you didn't know how far you were in over your head. But to be honest, I was already planning to come for you, B. It was time." His heartfelt words were all it took to send her over the edge. Great gulping sobs came from nowhere, making her feel as though she'd been steamrolled by her own emotions.

Luke slid his arms under her knees and behind her back, lifting her as if she weighed nothing at all. Walking out onto the shaded deck, he settled her on his lap and simply held her close. He remained silent, allowing her to vent all the pent-up emotion of the past few weeks. Her life had spiraled out of control, and she had no one but herself to blame. The last thing she remembered was burrowing her tear-stained face into the side of his neck and letting her mind float back into the blissful oblivion of sleep.

LISTENING TO BROOKLYN'S broken sobs was one of the hardest things he'd ever done, but she needed to cleanse all the negativity before she could begin the journey he had planned for her. He didn't offer platitudes he knew she wouldn't welcome, he simply sheltered her. This was a rare display of fragility, but she needed to purge the destructive emotion, so they started with a clean slate. Several heart-wrenching minutes later, Luke felt her sag against his chest. Leaning her head back so he could look into her red-rimmed eyes, he kissed her forehead.

"Even now you are the most beautiful woman I've ever laid eyes on, baby. Your anguish nearly broke my heart, but I'm grateful you trusted me enough to see you through it." She needed to know he would always be her shelter in the storm. "I want you to eat something, then we'll settle you out here in the breeze for a nap and let the healing power of the ocean work its magic." When she nodded, he lifted her and moved inside.

"We're going ashore to the cantina with the McCalls this afternoon. It's important we establish a bit of rapport with the staff and locals—it'll go a long way to ensure their loyalty later. This is a very close-knit community... they protect those they consider their own." Setting her at the table, Luke propped her injured leg on a pillow covered chair before dishing up their lunch.

"I see you already set everything up. I'm sorry my meltdown delayed your plans." Luke had moved into the small kitchen, but he leaned back around the corner, so their gazes met.

"I knew this was coming, B. We've been friends too long for me to not know where your thresholds are. That was part of the reason I was so desperate to get to you, I knew how close you were to the edge." Moving back until he could once again squat down until they were eye-to-eye, Luke took her hand in his. "You're mine, B. You have always been mine, you've just been too frightened to admit it, but we're going to fix that, I promise."

Giving her a sweet kiss, he fought the urge to push for more and moved back into the kitchen. Making drinks to serve with the food that had been delivered earlier, Luke kept her engaged in conversation, fearing he might well find her asleep if he didn't keep her talking.

"We won't stay ashore more than a couple of hours— just long enough for Cat and Cooper to add a few more security features to the area. They'll be arriving in about an hour, so they'll have time to unpack and set up before we make our way to the cantina. As a couple, we're going to befriend the folks in both cabins, but we'll only spend time with one or the other at any given time." He didn't explain the reasoning, she was fully capable of figuring out one team would always be standing guard over all three bungalows.

"What kind of goodies did Ian McGregor send along?" It didn't matter Brooklyn had tried to sound professional, he'd still heard the underlying respect in her voice. Brooklyn Adler might be a gadget addict of the first order, but Luke was probably one of the few people who knew she'd always aspired to work in Ian's Research and Development Department. He'd recently mentioned it to Mitch and been surprised to learn Ian had already been making inquiries about Brooklyn. After all, who better than to beta test security equipment than a thief.

"I know he sent heat and light sensitive security equipment that will link to Jace's office at Club Isola as well as the control center at Prairie Winds." He'd already passed along the extra bit of information she'd shared this morning about Mendoza, and until they got more information on the man's background or solved the mystery of the amulet, the team wasn't going to take any chances.

"Your brother has also hired extra security for your siblings and Dr. Monroe." When he stepped back into the room, he was surprised to see unshed tears glittering in her eyes. He raised a brow at her in question as he set the glasses down.

"I'm so sorry for all the trouble. If I'd pulled the plug on the retrieval when my gut told me to, none of this would have happened. This mess is costing everyone a lot of time and money."

"Say what's really on your mind, B. You've said you were interested in learning about Dominance and submission, we'll consider this your first lesson. Communication is key to any successful D/s relationship—always. Don't assume I can always hear you. Even if I could, there will be many times it's even more important to *you* that you are able to articulate your needs. Being forced to put things into words—to explain them to another person answers the questions in your own mind as well." He wasn't sure she was convinced until she took a deep breath and nodded.

"I don't like all the attention. I've worked under a cloak of anonymity for so long... it's... well, it's all I know. Staying in the shadows is my comfort zone." Her words had been firm, but Luke knew Brooklyn well enough to know she wasn't as confident as she was pretending to be. He didn't agree with her, but trying to convince her she was more of an exhibitionist than she realized would be wasted effort.

"Understood, but I think it's important to remember you are the only one concerned about the costs. No one— and I do mean no one else has batted an eye because there is no way to put a price on your wellbeing. Are we overreacting? Maybe. We all hope so, but we won't take chances with your safety, baby." She still looked frustrated, but at least she wasn't arguing. Lifting her into his arms, Luke moved back to the large bathroom. "Come on. I'll let you freshen up, then I'll help you change into one of the swimsuits your sisters sent."

Luke smiled to himself while he waited for her to call for him. Once he'd seen the clothes B's sisters picked out for her, he'd quickly texted Tobi West to ask her to send them a gift basket from the Forum Shops. He'd cautioned her to not send anything too kinky, but he doubted his words would sway the woman at the center of everything good at The Prairie Winds Club. The specialty shops Tobi and her best friend/business partner, Gracie opened behind the club had been so wildly successful, they'd become consultants to help club owners all over the country duplicate the concept with local as well as national vendors. Club members enjoyed having a safe place to shop for quality products, knowing their pictures wouldn't be splattered all over the internet by some fool with a cell phone.

Brooklyn's softly muttered curse brought him back to the moment, and without knocking, he opened the bathroom door to find her trying to balance on one foot while smearing sunblock over her exposed skin. Two competing thoughts crashed head-on in his head, and for a couple of oxygen stealing seconds, Luke forgot to breathe.

Undressing her for bed had been a test of his resolve, but he'd focused on one small expanse of exposed skin at a time. But this—fucking frozen hell—this was mind melting. Seeing her standing naked in front of him set his every protective instinct aflame. One side of his brain was screaming, *Mine!* while the more civilized side realized all the ways she was endangering herself, and she hadn't asked for help despite being instructed to.

Wrapping his hands around her slim waist, Luke frowned when he noted he could almost close the gap between his fingers. Lifting her, so she was seated on the counter, he smiled when she hissed—it served her right to have her bare ass on the cool stone top.

"You're lucky it's cold meeting your bare ass rather than my palm heating it up. I know you heard me tell you to call me when you were finished, so this act of deviance is being noted, B. I'm keeping a tally, so you'll want to be very careful that mile-wide streak of independence you love to wave like a red flag doesn't write checks your lovely ass can't cash." He was pleased to see a flush color her cheeks, but he wasn't fooled by the momentary sign of capitulation. Earning Brooklyn Adler's submission wouldn't be easy, but it would be all the sweeter for the struggle.

Chapter Eleven

STRETCHING HER SORE muscles, Brooklyn was grateful for the comfortable lounge chair Luke pulled into the shade for her. Keeping her sheltered from the worst of the sun, yet able to enjoy the gentle ocean breeze made the spot perfect. The lapping of the water against the support posts beneath the bungalow was lulling her to sleep despite the way her mind kept spinning around everything that had happened over the past few days.

Luke's words in the bathroom—before he'd helped her into the sorry excuse for a swimming suit her sisters had picked out—were still ringing in her ears. Good God, what had her damned sisters been thinking? Hell, she knew exactly what they were thinking. They'd been trying to play matchmaker for years. The Adler women all loved Luke and had never made any secret of their desire to see him join the family. Her brothers hadn't been as blatant, but they all liked and respected Luke as well.

Brooklyn had fallen in love with Luke the second week of their freshman year. She'd seen him standing in an alcove, listening as one of the school's janitorial staff cried about the recent loss of her husband. The older woman's family had returned to their own homes out of state, and she'd been left alone in a home that was suddenly far too quiet.

Later, Brooklyn learned Luke had heard the woman's anguish as he'd walked down the hall. He'd risked enraging a professor known for his strict attendance requirements to spend time with the grieving widow rather than going to class. He'd later explained the new widow had been devastated when she realized the world seemed to be continuing as if nothing had happened while her world had fallen apart. Brooklyn stood by, watching the sweet woman sob for several heart-wrenching minutes before noticing the professor whose class Luke missed was standing beside her.

"Is that your lab partner?" Brooklyn had been surprised and impressed he'd remembered their pairing earlier in the week.

"Yes. I was annoyed he missed class today, but now... well, now I'm very humbled. I should have waited to ask why he wasn't there." It had been the truth, she'd been pissed knowing she'd have to share her notes and bring him up to speed. Their advanced class was going to progress at a cut-throat pace that would... as the professor had said, "separate the cream and milk" very quickly.

"Then I think we've both learned a valuable lesson today, Ms. Adler. I want the two of you in my office at four o'clock." He'd turned on his heel without another word, leaving her gaping after him as he strode down the hall, turning her attention back to Luke and smiling as the older woman wiped her eyes and gave him a tight hug.

Brooklyn and Luke had arrived at the professor's office at four and been shocked to discover he'd ordered pizza.

He'd caught Luke up on the lecture and thanked him for the reminder of how important it is to not just look around you but to *see* as well. From that point forward, maintenance worker, Mavis Burke had become a very large part of their MIT Department. She'd been invited to their parties and included in every celebration, no matter how big and small.

Brooklyn was proud of her fellow graduates for continuing to keep Mavis close after leaving their alma mater. The elderly woman had been flown all over the country for weddings, christenings, even funerals. She'd retired and lived in a lovely retirement village near campus, so she could keep up with *her kids* in the Electrical Engineering and Computer Sciences Department. *Dang, her birthday is coming up... I need to make arrangements to send something.*

"Already done, baby. I took care of it last week. We sent something as a couple this year." Luke's voice sounded from her right, and the view of him leaning back in a chair, arms crossed over his bare chest stole her breath. She'd always been amazed at how remarkably fit he was, considering all the time he spent in front of a bank of computers. She'd seen pictures of some of the workstations he'd set up and envied his ability to fit an absurd amount of technology in such small spaces.

"Thank you. I would feel awful if she thought we'd forgotten her." Of course, Luke would never forget, he was the most organized genius she'd ever met. Most people with his I.Q. thrived on what they called creative chaos, but Luke had always been meticulous. His lack of response made her nervous, and when she finally met his gaze, the heat in his eyes caused her entire body to respond in a flash of heat.

"Tell me what you know about BDSM, baby."

His about-face caught her off-guard, but she shouldn't have been surprised. Brooklyn had known this discussion was coming for a long time. His interest in kink had been a sticking point for them for years, but not for the reasons she'd always given him. Hellfire and crispy critters, she hadn't had the courage to admit the truth to herself until a year ago.

Pulling in a deep breath, Brooklyn leaned back and closed her eyes. The way she saw it, she had two choices. Keep denying what he probably already knew and spend the rest of her life wondering what could have been... or she could own up to her interest in the D/s lifestyle and find out if any of the things she'd read were true.

"Talk to me, B. There isn't anything you can say or any question you can ask that will be off-limits."

This time when she opened her eyes, he was sitting much closer. Their eyes met again, and for the first time, she saw raw vulnerability and need. He'd always been so confident, it had never occurred to her Luke might doubt how much she cared about him. This time he shook his head and gave her a lopsided grin.

"You're wrong, you know. I don't doubt you love me, I've known it for a long time. But a large part of my love for you is my desire to see you as happy and fulfilled as possible. I want you to enjoy life to the fullest. I want to make all your dreams come true, baby. I won't stand idly by and watch you lock yourself away without ever taking a chance." The intense way he studied her might have been intimidating if she hadn't known how sincere his words were. When he leaned forward, steepling his fingers above where his elbows rested on his tanned legs, her brain cells scrambled.

Luke looked just as natural in board shorts as he did a tux—something she'd always marveled at. While it was true she was worried about damaging their friendship by becoming lovers, the real issue was her fear he'd walk away if she wasn't able to fully embrace a D/s relationship. Brooklyn's fear of disappointing him always made her feel as if someone had thrown buckets of ice water over her desire.

"My love for you isn't contingent on your acceptance of the lifestyle, B." She heard the frustration in his voice. Even though his expression hadn't changed, his gaze gave nothing away.

"What if I disappoint you?" Her question seemed to surprise him, and she wondered if he would call her on the fact she'd answered a question with a question.

"If you'll stop and listen to your heart, you'll know that isn't possible. You're surrounded by love, B. How is it that you have such a narrow view of an emotion you see every day? Take fear out of the equation, Brooklyn. Apprehension? Oh yeah, leave that one, but fear has no place between us. None. If you'll stop and think about it, you'll see I'm right."

She didn't have to stop and think, she already knew it was true. There was no one in the world she trusted more than Luke... *and no one else's opinion means more.*

"You're right, I want to try. I don't know much aside from what I've read. I went to a club with a group of friends once, but it was one of those meet and greet things, so we didn't get to observe any real scenes."

He'd already known about the trip almost a year ago. Several women had attended an open call evening intended to answer questions about the lifestyle at a club in New York. What Brooklyn had failed to mention was she'd been the one to drag her friends and sister out on a below freezing night to attend the event.

Most of the reputable clubs in the country were networked, so when Brooklyn's name showed up on the guest list, it triggered one of the hundreds of alerts he'd set up for her. Within minutes, he'd spoken with the club's manager, and from that moment on, he'd held the reins to what she'd been allowed to see. She was right, they hadn't seen much—that had been on purpose and by his design.

"What's your safe word, B?" Even without his empathic gifts, Luke would have known how his words affected her. He could see her pulse pounding a staccato beat at the base of her throat and how her blue eyes dilated until there was only a narrow ring of color surrounding the glittering black pupils.

"I'll use the stop light system. It's easy to remember and seems to be fairly standard." She was right about the universally accepted words in the kink community, but he needed to know she had a clear understanding of how and when safe words should be used.

"Tell me when you should use the words yellow or red, and I don't want a pat answer you memorized from a romance novel. I want to know what the words mean to you specifically." It wasn't going to be an easy question to answer when she didn't have any practical experience, but he wanted Brooklyn to begin the journey into introspection he knew would lead to unimaginable pleasure.

"Red stops everything, and I only use it if I'm in so much pain or drowning in emotions, I can't pull myself out of the quagmire. I'm supposed to use yellow if I feel myself sliding down a slippery slope, and I've forgotten how much I trust you."

His heart squeezed at her heartfelt response. She'd humbled him as much as he'd ignited an inferno that had been simmering for years. He'd kept his desires banked, waiting for the right moment—waiting for a sign from her she was ready for everything he had to offer, and she'd finally handed it to him in flashing neon colors.

"Your trust will always be my greatest treasure, baby. I'll hold it close to my heart and guard it with the same devotion I'll show your heart. You're safe with me, Brooklyn. You've always been safe in my care. If you stop and think back, you'll see a thousand ways I've shown you how much you mean to me." He saw a flash of something that looked too much like guilt move through her expression and shook his head.

"Don't. There is no place for guilt or regret in this discussion. You've shown me your love far more than you know. The late-night calls because you were lonely, the small gifts you sent from places all over the world, the texts to share a small victory or tear when something didn't work out the way you'd hoped—each one of those led us to this moment, B. Don't ever doubt how much you've given me."

Brooklyn had spent her entire adult life taking risks—bold leaps of faith most people would never attempt—so it baffled him why she was so reluctant to dance inside the fire when it came to her sexual needs. He'd known for years about the darker side of her desires, but she'd walked away from every opportunity he'd given her to open up to him. Luke was finished waiting, and he suspected she was relieved the chase was finally at an end.

"Above all else, remember everything I do is ultimately designed to bring you pleasure. You may not always understand the reasoning, you may not always enjoy everything we do, but I'm asking you to trust me." He was trying to disconnect from her thoughts out of respect for her privacy as she tried to get her feet under her. This discussion wasn't easy, but it was necessary, so Luke wasn't going to rush it.

It wasn't usually difficult to block thoughts, but it was more difficult with those he was close to and a huge challenge with Brooklyn, but it was virtually impossible to erect a barrier strong enough to withstand the waves of emotion pouring from her. The combination of anticipation and lust was intoxicating. Damn, she was going to test his self-control at every turn. He'd been waiting for so long, holding back wasn't going to be easy.

"We'll move at any pace you're comfortable with, baby, but once we start, we won't stop. We won't fail, you have nothing to lose and everything to gain." He'd spoken the truth and knew she sensed his sincerity when the last of the tension drained from her shoulders. Taking a deep breath that didn't seem to be enough to fortify the courage he knew was such a huge part of her, he looked on with tenderness as she pulled in several more calming breaths before giving him a tentative smile.

"I've wanted this for so long… and truthfully, it's not like me to be so hesitant when going after something I want, but I've never worried so much about failing either. I'd already been planning to make some big changes… in my life, I mean. I knew it was time." She took a shuddering breath, and he could see how much it was costing her to share the things he already knew or suspected.

Brooklyn had never seen her current occupation as permanent, but she'd never had a clear view of what she wanted to do after she stopped retrieving. He knew she'd had several offers, but nothing offered the same adrenaline rush she'd become hooked on. He hoped giving her another outlet for the rush would ease her transition to a less dynamic profession.

And baby, I know there are some very interesting offers headed your way.

Chapter Twelve

L UKE KNEW IT was time to distract Brooklyn from the spiral of uncertainty she was slipping into. For as long as he'd known her, she'd struggled with such an intense inner focus, she often forgot to look around and make sure the road she was watching so carefully still lead where she wanted to go. He often teased her about being a cartoon tracker... so focused on following the footprints of her prey, she didn't realize she was walking into the lion's den. He hoped to show her the benefits of looking up to enjoy the view.

"Let's begin, B. Loosen those handy ties at the side of your bikini bottom." She blinked at him in surprise, but he suspected it was more at his sudden change in direction than from the command itself. He knew she would hear the deliberate change in his tone. Her body responded before her mind caught up, proving he'd been right all along about the sweet submissive hidden beneath the bravado. There was a small piece of Brooklyn's heart that had always felt lost in the sea of her overachieving siblings. She often forgot how incredibly special she was, and he intended to remind her—repeatedly until she believed it.

Standing, he moved the short distance to squat down

beside the chaise where she lay. When he saw her shift, he shook his head. "Don't put any pressure on your leg, baby. Let me help you." When she tensed, he frowned. "You don't want to start this way, B. There is no shame or weakness in accepting help. And don't think for a moment my offer doesn't have a self-serving component. The quicker you're back on your feet, the faster we can increase the intensity of the pleasure. I can hardly wait to see you strapped to a St. Andrew's cross, your back, ass, and thighs bearing the scarlet marks of my flogger." When she shuddered, he gave her a lascivious grin.

"Seeing my marks on you will be fucking hot, baby. You'll swear every cell in your body is suddenly glowing with a warmth you can't identify, and when you surrender, I'll make you fly." His words weren't arrogance talking, they were the simple truth. She was his, and he intended to show her all the reasons they were perfect for one another.

Slipping his hand under her ass, Luke easily lifted her enough to pull the tempting patch of fabric out of his way. After setting it aside, he trailed his fingers from between her barely covered breasts down the center of her torso to the top of her bare mound before pausing to draw small circles over the smooth skin.

"Lasered?" She nodded, and he smiled. "Damn, you are fucking amazing. I'm going to show you how much I appreciate this, B. We don't have enough time right now for me to worship your body the way I want to, but I am going to give you the release I can feel stirring in your core."

Brooklyn's breathing was already becoming shallow, her breaths coming faster, hitching occasionally, letting him know how impactful his words were. As a Dominant, Luke understood the importance of incorporating the mind in seduction, but with extremely intelligent women, it was imperative. Since shutting down her rapid-fire thinking would never be easy, he planned to use those escalating thoughts to his advantage.

He let his hands caress their way slowly back up, curving around her narrow ribcage before slipping beneath the small triangles covering her peaked nipples. Pushing the fabric up, exposing the puckered, pink tips of her breasts sent a surge of blood to his cock, making him wish they'd set their lunch for later—much, much later. Rolling the sweet peaks between his fingers, Luke steadily increased the pressure until she moaned.

"You're everything and more. Your body responds so perfectly to my touch, we're going to set each other on fire, baby."

I'm not sure I'll survive it.

Her words echoed through his mind as if she'd spoken them out loud. He'd been watching closely, monitoring every nuance of expression and reaction, so he knew her words had come from inside. Luke wasn't going to intentionally monitor her thoughts, but he wasn't going to block her either.

Lowering his mouth over first one breast, then the other, Luke circled the outer areola with the tip of his tongue, savoring the first taste of her tender flesh.

"I'm going to light you up, baby. I'm going to make you come so hard, you'll wonder if you're coming apart at the seams. And when we get back to the bungalow later this afternoon, I'm going to start all over again."

"Please..." Luke wasn't sure she realized she'd spoken the silent plea aloud until she arched her back in silent invitation. "I need you to show me. I've waited so long. I want to know what it feels like to have..." He felt her entire body stiffen when she realized what she'd just revealed.

"Have you ever had an orgasm, baby?" The moment he asked the question, Luke knew he'd made a mistake— he'd given her a perfect out, but he was going to wait to see how honest she'd be with him and herself before correcting his error.

"I think I've had them, but only when I've used..."

"Toys?" When she nodded slowly, he grinned. "I'm going to enjoy watching you use them, baby. I'm more than a little voyeuristic, and it'll be fucking hot as hell watching you get yourself off." Her cheeks turned a delightful shade of pink, and he was suddenly very grateful for the bag of goodies Sam and Sage slipped into the supplies they'd delivered. Watching Brooklyn masturbate with the slender vibrator he'd seen in the stash was going to be like throwing gas on a fire.

BROOKLYN WAS SKATING a fine edge between arousal and paralyzing fear. She knew Luke would never do anything to hurt her—but she was terrified of disappointing him. And even though she'd finally confessed she wanted to try... she couldn't help but wonder if her body wasn't racing too far ahead of her head.

Luke's mouth felt molten as he sucked her throbbing

nipples against the ridged roof, pressing the tender flesh flat that sent bolts of electricity arcing between her breasts and her core. Lapping them alternately kept her mind whirling with need as cool air abraded the damp skin of one, then the other. She'd read about women who swore they could orgasm simply from having their breasts played with, and suddenly, those claims didn't seem nearly so outrageous.

Tossing her head side to side as the pulsing in her sex synched with Luke's worship of her breasts, Brooklyn felt as if a storm was gathering in her sex. The thought had barely whispered through her mind when she felt a surge of sexual energy she couldn't identify but knew it had come from outside herself.

"Come for me, baby." Luke's words were punctuated by his fingers slipping between the slick folds of her sex, pushing deep, expertly pressing against her G-spot, setting off an explosion of pleasure.

Colorful lights burst behind her eyelids, reminding her of fireworks displays she'd seen around the world. No matter where her family had been living at the time... Independence Day was always a huge celebration. Her parents believed they and their children were blessed to call the United States home and made certain to instill the same respect in their own children. Her dad always reminded them... those who have been given so much have an obligation to give back in equal measure. Luke's soft chuckle from beside her re-centered her scattered thoughts and Brooklyn cursed under her breath.

"I'm going to have to step up my game if you can still think after an orgasm, but I'm up to the challenge. It's damned humbling to have a sub thinking about her parents and patriotism when my fingers are still knuckle deep in her soaking pussy."

Brooklyn was shocked by the white-hot slash of jealousy she felt at his words. Why hadn't she considered he would move on while she continually pushed him to the side? It was hard to believe she'd been so naïve, but it was obviously true.

Luke withdrew his fingers, licking them clean. She banked her surprise before he saw it reflected in her facial expression, but when he arched a brow, she knew it was too late.

"I'm not going to deny I've played with subs at various clubs, baby. Continually learning and expanding my horizons is important to me—both professionally and sexually. I wouldn't have ever felt ready to claim you if I hadn't learned all I could, B. You're too important to have any detail left to chance."

Brooklyn knew the words were supposed to smooth her ruffled feathers, but they didn't keep her from wondering how many women he'd given mind-blowing releases to in the past? Before she could slide any further into her own head, Luke squeezed the tips of her tender nipples between his fingers.

"Stop! Don't do this. Focus on what is between us, not the submissives whose names I couldn't remember if I tried. Don't worry about anyone else. If you are continually looking backward, we're going to bump into a lot of obstacles we could easily avoid."

AUSTIN ADLER STOOD with his feet shoulder-width apart, staring out the floor to ceiling windows of his twenty-fifth-floor office, shaking his head. How the hell did his siblings get themselves in so much damned trouble? Brooklyn had managed to incite a man as close to certifiable as they came, Cat was shacked up with a *former* CIA operative who was anything but former, and London was working on some super-secret pharmaceutical discovery he strongly suspected her employer wasn't sanctioning.

He'd stayed at the office to tie up a few loose ends but lost track of time, not even realizing the sun had set, looking out where he knew the twinkling lights were boats rather than the cars and trucks lining the streets below. He missed spending time on his yacht. Hell, he couldn't remember the last time he's taken her out. His sisters teased him about it being a love boat, but nothing could be further from the truth. He rarely took anyone along, and when he did, it was one of his brothers.

"You're here awfully late, brother mine." He hadn't heard Asia enter but wasn't surprised she was also still at the office. As the corporate attorney for Adler Oil, Asia worked as hard or harder than he did. "When was the last time you took a day off?" Turning slowly around to face her, Austin crossed his arms over his chest and raised a brow at her in question without answering. "You work all the time, I'm tired of seeing you look longingly out the window as if you're a prisoner here. All work and no play make Austin a dull Dom, you know."

"A fact you wouldn't have discovered if you hadn't been at Dark Desires yourself." He'd been shocked to find his sister standing in the entry of his favorite kink club, and even more surprised to discover she'd been a member for over a year without him finding out.

The rules and closed-mouth culture of the club had changed very little after Cameron Barnes turned over the day-to-day operation to managers. The strict confidentiality agreements were ironclad and enforced with steel if they were breached, but he'd still been shocked to his toes to find out she'd flown under his radar for so long.

"I work hard. I play hard." Asia's casual shrug didn't fool him. His sister was still reeling from a bad break up over a year ago. She wasn't dating as far as he knew, and it was past time for her self-imposed social exile to end. The only time he'd seen her attend anything other than a business meeting was the night at Dark Desires, and she'd left within minutes of his arrival.

Studying her, he was surprised to see small submissive tells he'd never noticed before. Under his scrutiny, she shifted in discomfort and looked away. If she was sexually submissive and didn't have an outlet for the never-ending stress and frustration of her highly demanding career, Asia was headed for a crash—probably a significant one. Reminding himself he didn't get involved in his family's lives unless it was a matter of safety, he'd let it ride—for now. Deciding a change of subject was in order, he moved to his desk and drummed his fingers atop a small stack of folders on the corner.

"Have you looked through the applicants for my new administrative assistant?" His current right-hand was leaving in less than a month, and Austin had no idea how he was going to survive the transition. Eleanor Shaffer had been with Adler Oil since day one and was probably as capable of running the business as he was. She'd worked for his dad for several decades, but recent health issues were forcing her to scale back so much, he was going to need additional help. He suspected the older woman had finally found a way to force him to make a transition he'd been dreading.

"I did. They are all good candidates, and all passed a thorough background check."

He sensed there was more, so he didn't respond. He knew Asia had watched the interviews from behind the two-way mirror in his office and assumed she'd seen something he hadn't. It was unlike her to be so hesitant, making him even more curious about what she had to say.

"I should let you make up your own mind... after all, you'll be the one spending time with whoever you choose."

"But?" He was becoming more and more interested as the seconds ticked by. *Who the hell is this hesitant woman, and what has she done with my sister?*

Chapter Thirteen

WALKING INTO THE small beachside café, the first thing Brooklyn heard was a familiar female voice.

"I'm telling you, historians in the future are going to cite the removal of salt from butter as the beginning of the end. Western civilization teeters in the balance... you just wait and see." Brooklyn couldn't hold back her snort of laughter at Jen McCall's outrage and noted Luke seemed equally amused.

"You can't say I didn't warn you. She worked for the State Department before joining the Prairie Winds team, speaks more languages than anyone should know, is whip-smart, and a wild card. It takes both Sam and Sage to keep her in line." He felt her disapproval at his words and chuckled. "Those are their words, not mine, and they love her more than life itself, so it's not meant to be disrespectful. Jen tends to rush in where angels fear to tread."

"She sounds fun." *And maybe little scary.*

"You're right—on both counts." His answer came just as they reached the table, so she didn't have a chance to reply. It had been so long since they'd spent any significant quality time together, she often forgot how much stronger the connection was if he was touching her. He'd pressed his warm palm possessively against her lower back as they'd made their way across the café's length, so there was little doubt he'd heard everything she hadn't said. *Damnable gifted man.* She saw his lips quirk and shook her head.

"Hey neighbors, have a seat. We've been sitting here bemoaning the fall of Western Civilization." Sage's lighthearted greeting was spoken loud enough for anyone in the eatery to hear, and several of the patrons smiled knowingly. Evidently, they hadn't heard Jen's entire tirade.

"Laugh if you want to, but I know I'm right. Butter was smooth and tasty before. This watered-down, lame-as... all get out version is an abomination." Sam shook his head at her and held up his index finger.

"That's one, pet." Turning to Luke, Sam asked, "You finish that app yet?" When Jen sat up straighter, Brooklyn note a flash of worry move over the other woman's face before she saw Sage wink in her direction. "The punishment calculator we talked about? I'm getting tired of carrying around reams of paper."

"Ha ha. You're a real comedian, husband number one." When she rolled eyes and leaned back against her chair, Sam twisted a long lock of her hair around his fingers before fisting the silken strands to pull her close.

"That's two. I suggest you remember your manners, pet. Guests will not save your luscious ass from my wrath." Brooklyn felt her own breath catch before noting there wasn't any real anger in his tone, but he'd left no doubt in her mind their D/s relationship extended beyond the bedroom. Sam McCall was a Dom to the depths of his soul.

When she finally tore her gaze from the scene playing out in front of her, Brooklyn realized she'd unconsciously shifted away from Sam and into the shelter she felt with Luke. Sage McCall must have sensed her unease because he turned to her, shaking his head and smiling.

"I can't take them anywhere anymore. Ever since Suzie started pre-school, the two of them have been tangling like a couple of pissed mama bears. I swear, my sweet girl is going to grow up all confused about which one of them is her real mother. Wasn't there some kids book about a little bird looking for his mother?"

Brooklyn stared at him in disbelief. Could he really be making light of the tension surrounding them? Wasn't he going to do something to help his wife?

"B, Jen is not really in trouble—or at least, not anything she can't handle. She doesn't need Sage to save her. I assure you, she is perfectly capable of saving herself." Luke's words reassured her, and when she heard Jen fussing at Sam, she felt herself relax.

"Look what you've done. You've scared B, and now she thinks you're an oaf. Of course, you are an oaf, but you usually do a better job of concealing it. I think perhaps you're slipping in your old age."

Brooklyn liked the way Jen McCall's sparkling blue eyes reflected her quick sense of humor. Yes, indeed, this was a woman she could be friends with. Sucking in a breath, Brooklyn suddenly realized she had no idea how to be friends with anyone outside her own family.

Luke's hand slid over her knee, giving her a firm squeeze. She wasn't sure if the move was meant as a warning to not let her thoughts spiral out of control or if he'd been trying to comfort her. *Both*. She jerked in response to the single word that had whispered through her mind. *Fucking jumping jelly beans, did he just speak into my head?* Her mind was racing with possible explanations, grasping any thread... no matter how thin. It wasn't possible. Was it?

FOR THE FIRST time in his life, Luke was struggling to concentrate on two conversations at the same time. Hell, by the time he was in grade school, he'd mastered the art of tracking multiple conversations without missing a beat. He'd always hoped they'd be alone when she made this discovery. He'd deal with her fear of their enhanced connection later. He didn't want this to derail the progress they were making and send her running.

The last conversation Luke had with Brooklyn's mother had been over coffee early one Spring morning. He'd been scheduled on an early flight home and was pleasantly surprised to find her sitting in the kitchen with a cup of coffee ready and waiting. Season Adler had been an ethereal beauty, Luke always thought she shone from the inside out.

In every photograph he'd ever seen of her, Season had always looked exactly the same, she'd never seemed to age. She'd reminded him of pictures he'd seen of the flower children of the 1960s. Luke had sensed Season's gifts the first time they'd met, but she'd neither confirmed nor denied his unspoken questions—questions he was certain she'd heard or at least sensed.

As the mother of ten, Season was well accustomed to making the most of a few moments alone with someone she wanted to talk to, so she hadn't wasted any time getting to the point.

"Each of my daughters has inherited *the gift*. The women in my family have passed it down in varying forms for more generations than we can trace." She'd paused, waiting for him to ask, but he hadn't needed to, so she'd continued. "The gifts in our family are tied to love... true, soul-deep love that is only found once in a lifetime. It blooms in that fertile soil, but withers and dies if it isn't properly nourished."

To this day, Luke could still remember the way energy had seemed to sparkle around Season as she'd spoken. The hair on his arms and the back of his neck had stood straight up—it was a feeling he'd never experienced before or since. They'd talked for several minutes before she'd stood and walked him to the door.

"The next time I see you, everything will be so much different. Take good care of Brooklyn. She is going to need a steady hand to bring her back from the edge. Don't let her slip into the darkness that will tempt her." Season hugged him goodbye and sent him on his way without giving him a chance to ask what she'd meant—and less than a month later he'd gotten the call—she and Matthew were gone. Her softly spoken words often drifted through his mind at random moments, and more than once, he'd sworn they'd been accompanied by a faint rustle of air he couldn't explain.

Forcing himself to refocus on the conversations surrounding him, Luke was pleased to see Brooklyn was distracted by Jen's infectious sense of humor. He'd been certain they'd like one another and had been grateful Jen had been available for this assignment.

"She never ceases to amaze me." Sam's comment made Luke smile. "There is something magnetic about her—she draws people in. I've never met anyone who didn't feel it."

Luke knew it was true, even the man who'd targeted her had done so because he'd wanted her for himself. Turning his attention back to Luke, Sam's expression became serious.

"The intel coming in on Mendoza isn't good. He's got a lot of feelers out and doesn't appear to care how secretive his inquiries are. The chatter on the dark web is ramping up as the cash reward increases."

"Has Ian made any progress solving the damned puzzle?" Looking between Sam and Sage, Luke got the feeling there was something up, but he wasn't sure exactly what they weren't saying.

"Not yet, but he's bringing in some help." Sage's grin was positively sinister, and Luke couldn't hold back his chuckle.

"Talk to me. The fact you look like Snidely Whiplash makes me more than a little curious."

"Phoenix and Aspen Morgan should be landing in DC within the hour." Luke felt his eyes widen in surprise. Phoenix Morgan was one of the world's best game and puzzle designers. He'd been a millionaire before he was out of high school, and the wife he shared with Mitch Ames was well-known as a top-notch military analyst. It had been her affinity for strategizing Phoenix's games that led to their meeting. Online, Aspen's *Athena* persona was balls to the wall, but in person, she was much more sedate.

"And for good measure, he's flying Abby in as well." Luke had only met Abby Garrett once, but her reputation in the research and development of renewable energy had made her a strong contender for a Nobel Prize a couple of years earlier. Her older brother, Jace, was one of the few in Ian McGregor's inner circle, their friendship going all the way back to their youth.

Luke felt his eyes widen in surprise—hell, if the group Ian was assembling couldn't solve the amulet's mystery, it wasn't going to do Mendoza a damned bit of good to try. He was grateful for everyone's help, and it took him a few seconds to recenter himself as emotion threatened to steamroll him. The roller coaster ride of the past week had sapped his energy in ways he'd never experienced before, and he knew they were far from being in the clear.

"Any evidence Mendoza's traced us here?" Luke would have liked to believe Sam and Sage would have led with that information, but he'd learned to always double check when dealing with team members. They were the best at what they did and often assumed those who didn't share a military background saw things the same way they did, despite Luke's continued insistence it wasn't true.

"No, but we all know even the best alerts aren't fool-proof. Mendoza has a vast and impressive network, and he's damned smart. He prefers to fly under the radar for the most part. He recently purchased an island in the Caribbean, but we haven't been able to determine what he's planning to do with it." Luke would bet his sizable fortune the team had a damned good idea, but they weren't going to make an accusation without something more concrete than the rumor mill to back them up.

Sage's words didn't offer much comfort. Luke wasn't sure why the man's planned use for a land purchase was even being discussed—and it renewed his concern he wasn't keeping up on the latest intel. A plan started rolling around in Luke's mind, but until he had the chance to sort it all through, he wasn't going to throw the idea out on the table.

"I recognize that look." Jen's teasing voice brought him back to the present. "He has an idea and isn't sharing." She rubbed her palms together, reminding him of a mad scientist cartoon character. "Where are my bamboo shoots? Someone start the hot coals and fetch my tongs. I'll find out what's floating around in that genius mind of his. Your secrets will be revealed."

"Jesus." Sage's exaggerated eye roll made Brooklyn giggle, and Luke thought it was the single sweetest sound he'd ever heard. But then again, he might be wrong because her soft gasp as he slipped his fingers beneath the hem of her sundress sent a bolt of fire from his head to his cock, scrambling the few brain cells still receiving oxygen. Christ in heaven, when did he lose control of his damned cock?

It was time to head back to the cabana and play a bit with his sweet sub. Luke could already see she was beginning to bounce back, and since she'd agreed to try, he didn't want her to think he'd changed his mind. The roles they were playing made it was easy to make a quick exit. No one in the cantina would expect a group who'd just met to spend the entire day together, so they quickly finished up their drinks and said their goodbyes.

Pushing the state-of-the-art wheelchair out into the

bright afternoon sun, Luke walked into what felt like a wall of malevolent energy and realized too late he'd just come face to face with one of the men who'd shot Brooklyn at the edge of Mendoza's estate. The man nodded, but quickly pushed past him to get into the cantina. Luke hurried toward the cart they'd left parked at the end of the wide boardwalk before the man realized his mistake.

"What's wrong." Brooklyn's whispered question let him know she'd sensed the change in his mood. Gone was the barely restrained passionate lover who was rushing her back to their bungalow for a few hours of wild monkey sex. The lover had morphed into a man determined to protect the woman he loves.

As he turned the cart onto the boardwalk, Luke's phone started vibrating in his pocket. All three McCalls ran past them, with Jen taking a surprising lead despite her clear height disadvantage. Hell, the five foot nothing blonde bombshell looked like a damned Olympic track star. Since he hadn't been wearing any sort of communication device, his alarm had routed through his phone, delaying it several crucial seconds. Slowing to change directions, he muttered several colorful curses, choosing to vent his frustration on the technology rather than his snowballing fear. *Fucking hell, this shit has to change.*

Chapter Fourteen

C ATALINA LEANED AGAINST the doorframe, looking out over the water and wondered how she was going to survive being stuck in a tiny bungalow with Cooper Hicks. Everything about the man either made her insane with frustration or desire... there didn't seem to be anything in between. She'd known him for several years, but one stolen night of blazing hot passion had changed everything between them. One night, when she'd still been lost in the grief of losing her parents, she'd let her common sense be overruled by her loneliness. One night been all it had taken to plant the seed of desire that continued to draw her to Cooper and burrow itself in her psyche.

Cat had no personal experience with Dominance and submission until Cooper challenged her to let go of the tight reins she always held over herself. His explanation of power exchange had included a promise of a night she would never forget, and he'd delivered in spades. Cooper had changed her view of her own sexuality, and once it had been stretched to new lengths, it never recovered. She'd had sexual encounters with men she was dating in the intervening years, but nothing ever compared to the mind-melding connection she'd felt with Cooper. Damn it all to polka dot bunnies, she was going to kick her sister's ass for putting her in this position. As soon as B was back on her feet, they had a date in the sparring ring.

"It's awfully early for you to be so frustrated, Princess." Damned man could sneak up on a ghost. He moved like a jungle cat and was just as deadly. Reaching to where her fingers were sliding the silky fabric of her loose-fitting shirt between her fingers, he closed his fingers over hers, halting the nervous gesture she'd had since she'd been a toddler. It was one of her few "tells," and the only one she routinely had trouble controlling.

"I'm fine… just trying to figure out how a group of ancient Egyptians managed to snooker a group of the most brilliant minds in the country."

"Baffling, isn't it? And that's not even considering *the sum is greater than its parts* angle. The people Ian has pulled together play off one another, magnifying each other's intelligence. For those of us who are mere mortals, it's damned impressive to watch." It was easy to hear the admiration in his voice as he spoke.

Cat chuckled and shook her head at Cooper's humble observation. He wasn't fooling her, Cooper Hicks was brilliant and likely going stir crazy not being included in the think tank currently underway on Ian's private island. There was a reason the Agency wasn't letting him go easily.

"I checked all the electronics in Brooklyn's bungalow again. Everything is working, we'll know if a damned mosquito flies in. I'm just telling you now, I'm stealing all the tech you brought." Catalina tried to keep her tone light but suspected she'd failed when he slid the aviator sunglasses he wore down the bridge of his nose, locking her in place with a hard look. The ensuing silence was too long and heavy with anticipation, but he didn't rush to respond.

"Contrary to what you may believe, Princess, I have no problem sharing my toys with you. I recall vividly how much I enjoyed watching you enjoy them. As I've told you on a number of occasions—you only need ask—nicely."

Cat felt her face flush and wanted to curse how easily he'd turned the tables on her... again. *Rat Bastard.*

THE DAMNED WOMAN was going to be the death of him. Catalina Adler was the most frustrating and bewitching woman Cooper had ever met, and he had absolutely no fucking clue what to do about her.

She'd been skating a fine line for the past couple of years, and he knew the Agency was pushing her to take on more and more. Expanding her role with any of the covert agencies she worked with shouldn't even be a consideration. At first, she'd done a great job of flying under everyone's radar, but with more and more smaller airports using facial recognition technology, she'd popped up in a couple of key cases lately. It wouldn't be long until her master of disguise routine was no longer effective enough to keep her from being identified. He hoped like hell she wasn't in some hell-hole country on the other side of the damned planet when it happened.

The sound of an approaching boat had them both pulling weapons from their waistbands and stepping back into the shadows of the deck's pergola. The fishing vessel was traveling too fast to be business as usual, and Cooper felt the hair on the back of his neck stand up straight as a fission of fear flashed in Cat's eyes, letting him know she felt the threat as well. The boat appeared to be headed straight for them, but at the last minute veered sharply to the left and began a wide arcing circle.

Cat stood rooted in place, staring down at the water below Brooklyn and Luke's bungalow, her puzzled expression turning grim. He followed her line of sight noting a trail of tiny bubbles leading under the structure. *What the fuck?* Hitting the alert on the com device he wore, advising the team they had a situation and needed back-up—*ASAP*.

Cooper only managed two steps forward before the small building exploded. Fucking hell, *exploded* might be too tame a term—the small bamboo and wood structure disintegrated. He'd managed to take Cat to the wooden deck before the worst of the debris showered them, but he was pissed as hell about the damned ringing in his ears. *God damn it, I hate that shit.*

CAT TRIED TO pull in a deep breath and had a flash of pure panic when her lungs wouldn't inflate. "Stay still, Princess." The fog in her mind was beginning to clear, but the warm brush of Cooper's breath over the sensitive shell of her ear sent an entirely new wave of thought-scattering heat through her. Damn his wicked self, anyway. Cooper's deep voice had been one of the things she'd noticed about him when they first met, and it still made her panties wet far more often than she'd ever admit.

"What..." She'd tried to ask what the hell just happened, but the single word inquiry was all she'd managed. *Air! I need some damned oxygen down here, Ace.*

"Hang on." He shifted some of his weight from her, and Cat sucked in enough oxygen for her brain to kick fully back into gear.

"What the fuck happened?" There was a part of her that knew the answer, but the question slipped out before she could pull it back. She wasn't as well-trained as Cooper, but she wasn't naïve either. Catalina knew someone had just sent her sister an unmistakable message... they knew where she was. Before she could get lost in her own thoughts as she tried to put together the pieces, Cat was pulled back to the moment by a strange sound rumbling through Cooper's chest.

"Holy hell on a half shell. Did you just growl at me?"

"Language, Catalina."

Is he kidding? A building just a few yards from us was blown to bits, and he's going to bitch about my word choice? Before she could smart off a witty retort she was sure would have only thrown gas on the fire, Cooper jumped to his feet and pulled her up with him. The sudden change of position after being pinned beneath his weight made her head spin. Grasping his forearms to keep from tipping over, she heard him curse despite the sound of blood rushing to her head.

Without missing a beat, Cooper lifted her into his arms and took off running through their small cabana. Shaking her head in a futile effort to clear her vision, Cat cursed herself for not considering their small bungalow might also disintegrate. Her forehead ached, and the feel of something trickling from her hairline down the side of her face made her wonder what she'd hit when Cooper tackled her. Realizing he was taking her away from the job she was there to do, Cat stiffened in his arms.

"Stop!" When he didn't slow, she struggled, trying to extricate herself from his hold, only to have him tighten his arms around her.

"Be still. You aren't ready to run yet. I'm not cutting you out of the action, we both need to get the hell away from here until the entire site is cleared. We won't be any good to anybody if we get ourselves blown up in some grand display of heroics."

Catalina felt like an idiot for not thinking it through first, and that only added to the fact she was pissed they'd been found. It was time to call Austin... as much as she trusted the Prairie Winds team, she trusted her family more.

Chapter Fifteen

Thirty-six hours later

AUSTIN ADLER STEPPED into his inner office without switching on the lights. Thanks to a genetic gift from his father's side of the family, he had no trouble seeing even the smallest details of his inner sanctuary, including the man sitting deep in the shadows. Israel Adler was a large man by any standard—standing almost six and a half feet tall and built like a linebacker, he drew attention simply by walking into a room.

"I see you found the good Scotch." The brief flash of white teeth was the only sign his younger brother had heard him. "When did you get back?"

"Why didn't you call me?" Anger pulsed around Israel in such strong waves, his aura shimmered vivid red. Austin didn't usually pay particular attention to the energy fields surrounding his siblings, rarely needing the additional information—he knew them well enough without making the effort, but deep red wasn't anything to scoff at, so he took note.

"I hired the best people I could. You were on the other side of the fucking planet, did you expect us to sit on our damned thumbs until you got back?" Austin moved around his desk, flipping on his bank of computers before turning his attention back to his younger brother. Israel's skills as a security specialist and tracker were top tier in anyone's book, but only members of their family fully understood the reason for his success. To say Israel Adler could rip out your throat wasn't taking literary license, it was the God's honest truth.

"Where are they?"

Austin shook his head and smiled because they both knew Israel was fully aware of where Brooklyn and Catalina were at any given moment. Leaning back in his Italian leather office chair, Austin propped his booted feet on the corner of his desk and scanned the notifications scrolling up the screen on his personal laptop.

"You know perfectly well where they are. Ask what you really want to know and stop playing games." Israel could ply his damned intimidation ware elsewhere—Austin didn't have the time or the inclination to deal with his brother's bruised ego.

"Get me onto the island. I want to see B and Cat for myself. I'll check out the place and make sure it's the safest option. I'm tired of hearing about this shit third and fourth hand. You should have called me."

And there it is. The real reason he's as growly as a bear with a thorn in his paw. Austin shouldn't have been surprised by the request, but he was.

Getting Israel on the island wouldn't be difficult, hell, Ian McGregor would probably enjoy the challenge of his brother's *inspection*. But easy or not, Austin wasn't in the mood to kiss his little brother's ass. *God damn it, I'm tired of this shit. I need a vacation—preferably someplace with a high-end kink club. Fuck, maybe I'll tag along to D.C. I'll check on my sisters, then see if I can find a willing submissive.* A scene or two—*or three* would go a long way to venting some of his frustration.

BROOKLYN LOOKED AROUND the spacious bedroom, marveling at the beauty surrounding her. The team protecting her opted to stay in two of the apartments connected to Club Isola rather than the more accessible suites of the resort located nearby. From what she'd gathered when they arrived a few hours earlier, the apartments had been used for employees until most had married and gotten their own places. She'd slept so much on the flight from Belize, she had only catnapped since, allowing everything to replay in her mind until she was emotionally if not physically exhausted.

"Christ, B, you're wearing me out. Shut it down already." Luke's words were muffled by the pillow he'd pulled over his head, but it was easy to hear the frustration in his tone. There were times she didn't mind knowing he could hear her thoughts... *serves him right to have his sleep disturbed.* "Now you're begging for a punishment, baby."

"My sister is right next door. You don't want her coming in here and going all Wonder Woman on you... nobody wants to deal with Catalina in the morning... seriously." Brooklyn couldn't keep the amusement out of her voice. Catalina Adler had never been a morning person. Most people avoided her like the plague until after she'd downed the better part of a pot of coffee.

"This place was designed and built by Ian McGregor. Do you honestly believe he didn't plan for Doms to be able to make their unruly subs scream without disturbing the neighbors?" Looking at the lump buried beneath the bedding next to her, Brooklyn saw his eyes dancing with amusement and wondered how he'd moved the pillow without her noticing. "Come. I want to take a shower and play. Every time I think I'm going to get to explore your delectable body, some asshat screws it up." She laughed to herself because his observation was an understatement of monumental proportions.

Before she managed to scoot to the edge of the bed, he'd pulled her into his arms and was striding into the master bedroom's enormous en suite. Brooklyn knew it was early afternoon and was looking forward to dinner with Ian and his team, but she was particularly anxious to get a bit of relief from the sexual tension that had been simmering between them far too long.

"Don't worry, B, we'll get to the tension relief right away, but then I'm going to spend the entire afternoon exploring your body—mapping every square inch, learning what you love and crave." The shower he carried her into was a glass and marble room… there was no other way to describe it. A bench lined one wall, making it the perfect place for her to sit with her leg extended along its length. With her injured leg in position, Brooklyn felt her breath catch when Luke held up a length of fabric she'd seen laying on the countertop.

"The great thing about Ian is how clever he is at hiding things in plain sight." Wrapping the fabric securely around her leg just above the knee, Luke threaded the ends through a hook she hadn't noticed recessed in the marble wall. She felt her sex become slick with her arousal and tried to slowly close the gap between her legs. "I won't let you hide from me, B. There is no place for embarrassment between us." Her face heated, and he smiled as the flush moved over her entire body. The intensity of his stare made her feel as if he was trying to crawl all the way into her soul.

"Baby, I staked a claim to a piece of your soul the first day we met, you just didn't know it. But more importantly, you claimed mine as well. Every smile, glare, joke, phone call, email, and text we've shared since has been leading us here." He hadn't missed a beat keeping up with her thinking, and in some ways, it made it easier for her since she didn't always have to figure out how to say the things she knew needed to be shared.

"I want you to talk to me, Brooklyn. It's important for several reasons." While he spoke, Luke's hands never stopped moving. His palms caressed the inside of her thighs, painstakingly slow passes up until the sides of his fingers were so close to her sex, she could feel the heat against the sensitive tissues before he removed the teasing temptation and slid them back down again. With maddening patience, he repeated the move again and again until her muscles were quivering in anticipation.

"All of those sweet moans and softly exhaled sighs are sexy as hell, baby. They tell me you crave my touch as much as I do yours. They go straight to my cock," he smiled at her, waggling his brows in the way he did when he was imitating the old Vaudeville comedians they'd enjoyed watching on late night television, "but I want to hear you tell me what you love."

Brooklyn had fallen under the spell of his whispered words and intimate touch. Each pass of his hands pulling her deeper and deeper until her eyelids slid closed and he head fell back on her shoulders.

"Please, Luke. It feels so good. I want you to touch me."

"I am touching you, baby."

"More. It's... this isn't... I need more." Brooklyn's body was responding in ways she'd never anticipated, the response steamrolling her before she fully understood what she was asking for. She hadn't seen him pull the handheld shower head from the wall, and the sudden pulse of warm water against her swollen sex launched her straight over the edge into an orgasm so strong, Brooklyn saw stars streaking against the back of her eyelids. Reaching out blindly for him, she grasped his shoulders, hanging on as if he alone could keep her from lifting off the marble bench.

WATCHING BROOKLYN SHATTER was the most erotic thing Luke had ever seen. He knew he had to get this first orgasm out of the way, or she'd never be able to focus long enough for him to play later. This one was pure release of pent-up emotion and energy, the intimacy he knew would seal their souls together would come later. While sexual release was a damned fine way to spend time, it wasn't what would make her his forever.

"You are so fucking beautiful, B. Your body is so responsive to my touch, we're attuned to the same universal beat. Our souls are already synching, our heartbeats aligning with one another." He spoke the truth, and even though she was still reeling from the powerful orgasm he'd given her, he was certain her heart was listening. Brooklyn was already his, he just needed to give her time to bring her mind, heart, and body into alignment.

Standing slowly, Luke used the showerhead to help Brooklyn wash her hair, carefully finger-combing the long strands before letting her watch as he quickly finished up his own shower. He was grateful for the never-ending supply of hot water and vowed to make sure tankless systems were installed in the new home he was building in New Mexico. His family had teased him when they'd heard he was building a mountain retreat, and he'd simply smiled and nodded at their humble assumptions. Their vision of a mountain cabin differed significantly from the reality of the cavernous concrete and glass structure nearing completion outside Taos.

The home had features designed by some of the most creative architectural minds in the country. His Uncle Mitch's friend, Bryant Davis spent over a year designing the engineering marvel that was modeled after the converted mine home he and three others built in the Colorado Rockies.

Luke managed to avoid all the entanglements with government mining bureaucrats his Uncle Mitch dealt with by utilizing a series of natural caves rather than abandoned mines. There hadn't been any real need for structural reinforcements, but Bryant had added them, anyway. The home was built to withstand almost anything aside from a direct nuclear attack. The place was also enormous, having been designed and built with the large Adler family in mind.

When Luke referred to the house as a mountain cabin, Bryant Davis had laughed out loud. "More like a mountain lodge." The home was slated to be ready for occupancy soon, and Luke was grateful work was continuing in his absence. The ShadowDance team in Colorado was installing the security system Ian designed, and Luke had taken a leap of faith and turned the interior design over to Tobi and Lilly West. For all their wild ways, the two women had impeccable taste and no reservations whatsoever about demanding quality workmanship. He'd heard they'd enlisted Catherine Lamont's help and laughed more than once, wishing he could be a fly on the wall during their brainstorming sessions.

"You accuse me of letting my mind wander, but I'm not sure you're any different. Who is Catherine Lamont?" Brooklyn's question made him chuckle. Not only was she confirming her mother's remarks about a legacy right, but for the first time, she'd shown a hint of possessiveness where he was concerned, and damned if that didn't please Luke more than it probably should.

"Daniel and Catherine Lamont are the parents of Alex and Zach Lamont, the owners of the ShadowDance Club. They also head up the ShadowDance team, a group of former Special Forces operatives very similar to the Prairie Winds group you already know about."

"It amazes me these teams exist, but from everything I've learned, they serve a very real purpose."

They'd talked about this more than once, and he knew

she'd been shocked to find out the groups were not only sanctioned by the United States government, but they were often contracted by several other countries as well.

"Do you think they would consider letting me help?"

Because of his gift, people were rarely able to surprise him, but Brooklyn managed it with one whispered question. He'd planned to play for a while after their shower, but this was an important shift in their conversation, and he immediately revised the plan he'd set up earlier.

Brooklyn had just blown open the door to a conversation he and several others were hoping to have with her after they were assured she was safe. This discussion might be sooner than planned, but he certainly wasn't going to complain. Anyone who knew Brooklyn Adler would agree, she was a justice seeker at heart. Given the chance to fight for what was *right*, their biggest challenge would be keeping Brooklyn from running headfirst into the flames.

Shutting down the shower, Luke grabbed towels from the warmer and wrapped one around her slender shoulders before drying himself and loosening the binding around her leg. Gently massaging the muscles, he made certain she didn't have any lingering effects from being tied open to his view.

"You liked being bound, didn't you, baby? I can't tell you how happy that makes me. I'm looking forward to playing with all sorts of bondage, but first, we're going to talk. You asked about helping, and I'm thrilled you're interested because I've got a few ideas along that vein."

Chapter Sixteen

A N HOUR LATER, Brooklyn found herself seated on a comfortable leather sofa facing a stone fireplace that looked like it should be in a Hallmark movie rather than the office of a kink club. Ian McGregor sat across from her, leaning back in a wingback chair, his fingers steepled under his chin, studying her with such intensity, she had to fight the urge to squirm.

"Your office is beautiful." She decided to skip the rest of her assessment, no need to tell the man how easily she could identify every security element he'd tried hard to disguise in the large space. She'd expected a polite acknowledgment of her compliment... what she got was a wicked grin, followed quickly by laughter.

"Yes, Brooklyn, I agree, but I'd very much like to hear what you didn't say." She must have looked surprised he'd read her. Shaking his head, he added, "Before you ask, no, I can't hear you in the way Mitch or Luke can, but I'm a Dominant and a good one, if I do say so myself, which means I'm adept at watching people. I understand the nuances of their body language, and even though you work very hard to cloak yours, it still shines through in your beautiful eyes."

She'd been looking just past his left ear while he'd been speaking, a trick she'd learned long ago to avoid direct eye contact while maintaining the illusion she was listening intently.

"Let me tell you what I see, then you can tell me what you find lacking in my office—deal?"

Brooklyn had dealt with her Dominant brothers enough to recognize a rhetorical question when she heard one, so she kept quiet and waited.

"I see a woman who works too hard. She's driven to the point of exhaustion by an inner need to succeed, but her definition of the term is far harsher than it needs to be. I see a natural submissive who'll blossom with the right guidance. Your Dom's biggest challenge will be making certain you take care of yourself."

Brooklyn felt her eyes widen in surprise as she met his gaze head-on and hoped like hell her mouth wasn't gaping open like a fish out of water. All she could do was blink while her mind scrambled to catch up. She was barely aware there were other people in the room, Ian McGregor's focus was so laser sharp, Brooklyn didn't dare look away.

"You remind me of my *Carlin*. I'm anxious to introduce the two of you, I believe you'll be friends. I'm certain the mischief you'll get into will give Luke and I plenty of opportunities to punish you, so it sounds like a winning proposition all the way around."

Chuckles from around the room finally broke the spell he'd managed to weave with his keen observations. Shaking her head, Brooklyn was wise enough to keep her denials to herself. *No need to start racking up punishments any sooner than necessary.*

"Now, we have visitors on the way, so we'll save the update on your safety until they've been cleared by Jace. In the meantime, tell me what you bit back earlier. Let's start with how long it will take you to retrieve an object I hid in this office early this morning. I'll spot you a full minute because of the crutches." This time his eyes twinkled with mirth, and Brooklyn wondered if his children had inherited their father's well-hidden sense of humor. Damned the man for knowing exactly how to play her.

Hopping to her feet much faster than any of them anticipated, Brooklyn was already on the move before Luke crossed the room to help. Waving him off, she set about pointing out all vulnerabilities as she passed them on her way to a safe she'd bet no one else in the room knew was there. Leaning down, she tapped around the edge of the inlaid wooden medallion in front of his desk, smiling when the entire piece lifted hydraulically before the right side flipped up showing metal steps leading down into a dark hole. Waving the tip of her crutch just beneath the floor, she smiled when motion activated lights sparked to life.

"Son of a bitch, McGregor. I've worked for you two years and didn't know that was there." A man at the side of the room she hadn't been introduced to gave her a nod then turned his attention to Luke. "She's a keeper, Grayson, take good care of her or someone else will." Luke gave the other man a slow nod.

"Always."

Maybe the conversation should have made her feel more like a possession than a person, but it didn't. There was an undercurrent of respect she appreciated so she turned her attention to Ian.

"If I had my tools, I'd be in and out of your safe in five minutes, ten at the most. I wouldn't take the bait to leave by the alternate exit, either." She flashed him a knowing smile when his brows rose in surprise. "The ventilation tells me there's at least one other exit, probably more. But I wouldn't use either. I'd have also disabled the motion lights before they ever kicked on because they're likely tied to the cameras."

Tapping the switch, she grinned as the entire thing righted itself, and in a few seconds, it looked as if it had never been disturbed. Moving quickly, she scanned the bookcase. Turning to smile at Ian, she noted the look of pride on Luke's face and felt her face heat. Lifting what looked like an antique child's bank, she grinned when the case opened revealing a small room. The bank had been an easy choice—a child's toy in a kink club office wasn't something she would miss.

"Ms. Adler, you are one amazing woman." This time she recognized the man who'd spoken. She'd run into Kalen Black almost a year ago, but she doubted he'd remember their chance encounter. She might not have recognized him when Ian introduced them earlier today if not for his distinctive voice.

Kalen Black had a presence she doubted many people—male or female—forgot. His voice was like warm buttered rum, and when she'd mentioned it to Catalina a few weeks later, her sister had laughed, telling her women on three continents cried when the man they called the Archangel of D.C. was taken off the market by Abby Garrett. Kalen's eyes sparkled with humor as he waited patiently for her mind to spin around inside her head, bouncing around like a damned pinball.

"God, I love brilliant women. They are a gift directly from God himself."

The door of Ian's office banged open, and a woman close to Brooklyn's size breezed into the room without waiting for an invitation. The petite woman's Native American heritage was clearly written on her perfect cheekbones and golden bronzed skin tone. The small woman zeroed in on Kalen Black, flashing him a saucy grin.

"I'm thrilled to know you love smart women, husband mine. I hear our guest has been settin' y'all straight on Ian's poorly done security. Too bad big brother wasn't here to eat some humble pie, you know how I love to see Indy squirm." Launching herself the last few feet, Kalen caught her easily, hugging her against his chest.

"Dammit, Short Round, I swear your men need to beat you more often—you're a hot mess." Brooklyn blinked in surprise as Jace Garrett strode confidently through the door, followed by her brothers, Austin and Israel. Brooklyn didn't realize she was holding her breath until Luke stepped up behind her, squeezing her shoulder, letting her know he had her back.

"It's just the two of them, B. I didn't know they were coming until a few minutes ago, or I would have warned you." She appreciated his whispered words but knew her brothers wouldn't have missed the barely audible words. *Damn dog ears anyway. Blah.* Austin laughed out loud while Israel glared as he stalked closer.

"What the hell, Brooklyn—if the family won't call me

when you are in trouble, I damned well expect you to do it yourself." And there it was, his nose was out of joint because nobody tried to track his happy ass down.

"I'm doing well, thanks, little brother." The muscle in his jaw ticked, and Brooklyn wanted to give herself a high-five. Why was there always a six-year-old lurking just beneath the surface who enjoyed gigging her brothers? Shrugging to herself, she felt Luke's amusement move through her mind, lighting up the dark corners with warmth and light.

When they were kids living at home, all ten Adler siblings had been thick as thieves. Moving so often meant they rarely had time to establish outside friendships, so they'd been one another's best friends. After their parents died, they'd each dealt with the grief in their own way, and sadly, it seemed they continued to drift further apart every year.

Israel stopped a couple of feet in front of her and opened his arms. Brooklyn didn't hesitate to accept what she knew was both an invitation and apology. Heading up one of the fastest growing personal security companies in the country, Israel Adler wouldn't have been at all happy to learn his sister was facing danger alone. As the next to youngest male sibling, Israel had always seemed to feel the need to prove himself. He worked harder than anyone Brooklyn knew, and she often worried he was going to let his life slip by without noticing.

All five Adler men were tall, and Brooklyn felt herself smile as she was completely engulfed in his hold. His hug calmed her in a way only family could, and she felt a familiar burn at the back of her eyes. Determined to not be controlled by emotion, she pulled back and smiled up at him.

"As happy as I am to see you, what are you doing here, Is?"

"I wanted to see for myself you're okay. It's not that I don't trust big brother, but..." Looking over to where Austin stood waiting, Brooklyn couldn't hold back her grin when he rolled his eyes at Israel's not-so-subtle complaint. "No one called me."

Brooklyn heard the layers of meaning in her brother's words... beneath his frustration was pain, and it made her sad to think he felt as though he'd been set aside. *It's not on you, B.* Luke's reassurance drifted through her mind, and Brooklyn began to really appreciate how intimate their growing connection felt.

"See, Indy, this is how sweet brothers do it. They show up and hug their sister, make sure she is okay, and don't pretend she's annoying when we all know she isn't." Abby's amused voice broke the spell, and Brooklyn was grateful for the emotional reprieve.

"God, you're a pain in my ass. I thought your men would have straightened you out by now—damned slackers." The room erupted in gales of laughter, making it difficult for Ian to restore order for several minutes.

Two hours later, the group had brainstormed until Brooklyn's head throbbed. They'd reviewed all the available information they'd gathered about other ancient pieces discovered to contain secret information but hadn't seen any of those same markers on the medallion used in the amulet. Rubbing her hand over her forehead in frustration, Brooklyn watched Abby pace in front of the wall of windows in Ian's office. It hadn't taken Brooklyn long to understand how Abby's mind worked—she needed to be moving in order to process, and it was fascinating to watch.

"You know, we don't have to solve the puzzle. We want to, but it isn't necessary." Abby's words brought everyone in the room to a dead stop. The sudden silence was almost eerie as attention focused on her. "We just need to make Mendoza believe we've cracked the code. I doubt he gives a rat's ass one way or the other about finding one of the most sought-after religious artifacts in history. He only cares about the money." When Ian started to speak, she held up her hand. "I know he can't sell information he doesn't have, but we can call his bluff. If he thinks I've found the answer, we can bait him."

The room erupted in angry voices of protest, but Brooklyn didn't let them draw her attention away from Abby. Watching the other woman closely, Brooklyn could have sworn she saw the pint-sized genius' lips twitch in satisfaction.

Oh yeah, she loves to cause chaos, and she's damned good at brewing up the perfect storm. I like her.

Chapter Seventeen

B ROOKLYN TUGGED ON the hem of the dress she was
almost wearing and shook her head. "It's too short.
Where'd you find this anyway, the kiddie section?" Luke
was leaning against the door frame, watching her fidget,
amusement lighting his expression, making it almost
impossible for her to maintain any semblance of anger.
"Damn it, Luke, you're screwing up my pissy mood."

"B, you love the dress, and we both know it. It's hot,
shows off your killer legs, and if you move just right, you'll
flash the room a tempting glimpse of the bottom curve of
your delectable ass."

Turning to face him, Brooklyn couldn't decide if he
was teasing her or serious. *Damn it, my brothers are going to
be at the club tonight. They do not need to see my pink bits.*

"Baby, I assure you, I have no intention of sharing the
view with your brothers—nor do I want you subjected to
watching them play. Boundaries and consent are equally
important in the lifestyle."

Brooklyn felt her shoulders relax and took a deep
breath for the first time since they'd left Ian's office.
Knowing he'd already taken everything into consideration
settled her nerves, and she regretted questioning him.

"Don't worry, B, this is new to you. I'd be more worried if you weren't anxious about your first visit inside a kink club where you know your brothers are also attending. Club Isola is big enough for all of us."

"Thank you for being patient. I know I keep saying I want to try... and I do, but it seems like I keep getting in my own way." Brooklyn forced herself to meet his intense gaze and was surprised to see his lips curved up in a smile. "If it's frustrating to me, it must be making you insane."

"Not at all. I've waited years for this, B. A few more hours or days are a small price to pay for finally being able to show you how good we're going to be together." He pushed away from the doorframe to step up behind her. Studying her in the mirror, she saw his eyes zero in on her bare neck. "I have something for you to wear tonight, baby. It isn't a permanent collar, but I don't want you wandering around the club without an outward sign you belong to me." She'd read enough about the lifestyle to understand the implication of being an uncollared sub in a kink club, and she breathed another sigh of relief knowing he'd already planned for her protection.

"Brooklyn, your safety will always be my number one concern. Your pleasure is a goal, but your well-being will always trump everything else."

She remembered him once telling her he felt the years she was spending as a retrieval expert would compromise her safety for years to come. At the time, she'd felt he was being paranoid, but now she wondered if he'd been right. When her mind returned to the present, she noted he was still watching her intently.

"Baby, I don't need to listen to the way your mind is

racing to see where you're headed. And yes, I still believe you'll face security issues for many years to come. That concern was one of the reasons I built the New Mexico house." Brooklyn knew he was building a home outside Taos, but she had no idea his worry for her safety had been an impetus setting the project in motion. "I can't wait to show it to you, but I want all the security protocols fully functional before we move in. There are some amazing features designed specifically for you."

Brooklyn stood silently, trying to process everything Luke was saying. In a lot of ways, her body seemed to be recovering faster from the disaster on Mendoza's island than her mind. The small parcel of land off the Northeast Coast, with its jagged rocks and unforgiving weather, had been a catalyst for so many changes. Even now, she often felt as if she was watching the world through a haze, distorting things to the point nothing was perfectly clear. *I really have to stop taking those damned pain meds.*

EMILIO MENDOZA WATCHED the conversation scroll up the oversized screen on the wall-mounted monitor, smiling to himself. He and his team had been monitoring the dark web continuously since they'd heard Ian McGregor was gathering some of the most brilliant minds in the country. Every one of the men and women gathered on McGregor's private island had a Mensa-level IQ, and several were well-known for their puzzle mastery skills.

Apparently, McGregor had gotten tired of trying to solve the puzzle himself and decided to bring in the big guns. If the chatter was to be believed, McGregor's effort had paid off. Emilio was surprised word had leaked out of his inner circle, but on the other hand, he knew too well how hard it was to keep employees from talking. Drumming his fingers on his desk, Emilio watched the screen as the only two people in the chat room discussed the excitement on the island and speculating on who would be sent to retrieve the "prize."

"Are you going to let them steal what belongs to you, Emilio?"

Looking up, he was surprised to see his mother standing near the door. He hadn't seen her in several days and had begun to think she'd returned to her own home without letting him know she was leaving.

"They will take the money and the credit. You'll be left with nothing but the memory of having the amulet stolen from you. I want to see your name in the history books, my son."

He watched her closely, knowing she had more to say. He could always tell by the way she studied him. She'd always been able to make him feel insignificant. No matter how successful he became, it was never enough to satisfy her.

"The thief made you look weak and foolish. What are you going to do about her? A thief whose family fancies itself wealthy should not be able to ruin the reputation you've spent years earning." He shouldn't have been surprised she'd learned the thief's identity, but he was. Obviously, the gossip among his inner circle was still a problem—he was going to enjoy making an example of whoever was talking to his mother.

"I know, mother. I am waiting for a call now. I hope to be on the island soon. Dealing with the thief will be a pleasure." Once he finished with Brooklyn Adler, no one would dare steal from him again. The warning would be well-timed to keep anyone from questioning him once his operation in the Caribbean was up and running. Not for the first time, Emilio wished his mother would butt out. If he was honest, she'd been a pain in his ass since long before she fell from her bedroom balcony.

Shaking his head, Emilio felt the tentacles of a migraine reaching out to sink their steel talons into his brain. Fumbling in the drawer of his desk, he searched for his medication before his vision became so blurry, he couldn't find it. When his fingers wrapped around the familiar bottle, Emilio jerked the lid from the top scattering pills over the surface of his desk. Swallowing two of the small, white tablets he knew would bring relief, Emilio moved to the supple leather sofa at the other side of his office. Ignoring his mother, he moved his hands to the sides of his face, using the heat to calm his racing heart and sent up a silent prayer she'd be gone when he woke up.

LUKE STARED ACROSS the room as the women in the corner leaned back their heads, laughing at something Aspen Morgan said. He wondered again what the hell he'd been thinking of bringing Brooklyn to the club.

"I'm not sure this was a wise decision. I was counting on Aspen to be a calming influence." Luke turned his attention to Phoenix Morgan when he heard the other man snort back his laughter. Shaking his head, Luke returned his attention to the women gathered in the semi-secluded alcove of Club Isola's large main lounge.

"I don't know what you've heard about my lovely wife, but assuming she'd be a calming influence was a mistake. *A very large mistake.*" Phoenix's eyes never left the wife he shared with his longtime friend, Mitch Ames, as he studied her with a mixture of amusement, love, and annoyance. "The word is spreading quickly over the dark web; our contacts have done a good job planting seeds in the right places."

"Mendoza only frequents a few chat rooms we're aware of, and he was logged in earlier today while a couple of the members were discussing the rumors. Best of all, neither of the principals were ours—they're both treasure hunters so Mendoza will be more inclined to take the bait." Ian grinned, and Luke would bet his considerable fortune the expression had given his mother nightmares.

"Have we ever gotten any more information on his mother? The last I heard there were questions regarding her death." Luke watched as Ian's expression turned thoughtful.

"About that—seems Mendoza has referred to her a few times in the only group he participates in. He is a member of several groups but is what the other members refer to as a stalker." Luke watched Ian's gaze lock with Callie's. He couldn't hold back his chuckle when his host lost focus on their conversation. For long seconds, Ian's attention was fully on the beautiful blonde weaving her way through the crowd. Clearing his throat, Luke managed to pull Ian's attention back to what he'd been saying.

"It seems Mendoza always refers to his mother in the present tense—as if she isn't deceased. He referred to a recent conversation with her in a comment not long ago." Ian held out his hand as Callie approached, his expression softening as she stepped close enough for him to tug her against his chest. "*Carlin*, you look beautiful, and I'm thrilled you've joined us."

"I'm sorry I'm late, our children were giving the nanny a run for her money, and I hated to leave until they were settled."

"You do realize we're paying her a rather substantial salary to handle them, don't you?" Ian's tone hadn't changed, but the pink flush staining Callie's cheeks told Luke this was something the two of them had discussed before—and from the electricity crackling around them, probably several times.

"Yes, Master. I'm sorry, and I'll graciously accept whatever punishment you deem appropriate." The twinkle in Callie's eyes changed to what could only be described as pure mischief. Luke couldn't hold back his chuckle at her blatant attempt to top from the bottom—a challenge everyone knew Ian wasn't going to let go unmet. Exhaling a deep breath in an audible whoosh, Ian set his lovely wife back at arm's length and studied her closely. After several tense seconds, Callie started to fidget, and Luke wondered how much longer Ian would make her wait before deciding her fate.

"Strip." Callie's eyes went wide before filling with unshed tears, but she pulled the dress she was wearing over her head and handed it to her Master. "Go find my bag and bring it to me, you have forty-five seconds, beginning now.

Every second you are late will add to your public punishment." She stood blinking at him as if trying to make sense of the words before Ian's voice boomed around them. "Now, Callie." She turned and darted into the throng of people surrounding them but wasn't making much progress.

"This place is so crowded, she doesn't have a snowball's chance in hell of meeting that deadline, Ian." Phoenix shook his head and chuckled. Callie reminded Luke of a small pinball bumping into people as she tried to hurry through the throng surrounding the bar. Callie was so petite, she wasn't making much headway against the crowd—most of whom made her look like a small child streaking through her parent's dinner party. "You're a bastard, Ian. It's going to take her sixty seconds to get to the bar, another thirty to find your bag and ninety seconds to return carrying it since I'm assuming you saw this coming and weighted it down." Ian's sinister grin confirmed Phoenix's observation.

"She's been working entirely too hard and has earned this punishment. Remember, what is punishment for one submissive is bliss to another. My *Carlin* is too sweet to ask for what she needs, so it's my job to watch her carefully and intervene when necessary."

Luke would have laughed at Ian setting Callie up if he hadn't felt her need when she'd first approached them. He was always amazed at Ian McGregor's ability to function on several levels at the same time without so much as blinking. Working with a team to solve an ancient mystery, coordinating the team protecting Brooklyn, and setting a trap for Mendoza hadn't kept him from noticing his sub's need. Club Isola had a well-respected training program for both Dominants and submissives because Ian had personally overseen the rigorous course for years.

Ian McGregor and Cameron Barnes set the bar high for every other exclusive club that followed. Mountain Mastery in Montana, The ShadowDance Club in Colorado, and The Prairie Winds Club in Texas had all benefited from Ian and Cameron's expertise and patient guidance.

"Christ, man, where did you go?" Sage's amused voice pulled Luke back to the moment, and he turned to the other man and shrugged. Sage shook his head and chuckled. "Damn, dealing with geniuses can be a real pain in the ass. This is why Uncle Sam keeps you all stateside behind desks, you'd get the rest of us blown to bits." This time it was Luke's turn to laugh out loud because everyone knew Special Forces soldiers were the military's cream of the crop, both intellectually and physically.

Phoenix snorted back a laugh and shook his head before speaking. "I'm not getting involved in that discussion, but I would like to point out one more thing before we retrieve our subs." Luke followed Phoenix's gaze, to the area where the women were sitting. They appeared to be getting restless which wouldn't bode well for anyone if it was allowed to continue. "Mitch is connecting with physicians and psychiatric contacts who might have treated Mendoza, or anyone closely associated with him, so hopefully we'll get some added insight soon."

Luke almost laughed out loud at the total PCBS Phoenix Morgan had just spouted. The man wasn't known for his business acumen for no reason. If Luke's Uncle Mitch was "connecting," it meant he was hacking the medical records of anyone who'd so much as seen Mendoza for a scratch. The man wouldn't have any secrets when Mitch was done. Before he had a chance to make his excuses and move away from where he'd been standing with the others, Brooklyn's voice moved through his mind.

"I don't know, perhaps he's changed his mind." Luke's attention zeroed in on the conversation, and he growled in frustration when he realized Brooklyn thought he'd changed his mind about showing her around. Damn it, he'd been so eager to find out where things stood with Mendoza, he'd neglected the real reason the two of them had come downstairs.

The other men were chuckling as he stalked toward where the women sat in a small alcove. The last thing he wanted was for Brooklyn to backpedal on her promise to explore the lifestyle with him. He planned to challenge Brooklyn's narrow view of her submissive nature, and he'd waited too long to fuck things up by letting her stew in her own insecurity. It was time to show her what he already knew—they were going to be perfect together, and the sex was going to be explosive.

Chapter Eighteen

BROOKLYN'S BREATH STUTTERED when she looked up to find Luke standing just outside the small nook where she'd been chatting with the other submissives. With his booted feet spread shoulder-width apart and heavily muscled arms crossed over his chest, straining the black fabric of his shirt, he sent her senses reeling. Heat spread through her as her body responded in the way it always did to him.

The memory of the blistering kiss he'd given her before they'd stepped through the secured door into the club made her lips tingle, and she raised her fingers to trace the fleeting feeling before it melted in the heat of the moment. For a man who spent the majority of his time in front of a bank of computers, Luke Grayson was ripped. His thick chest was a testament to his commitment to a rigorous weight training program. She'd seen the way women reacted to him, but he'd never seemed to notice.

You are fucking beautiful. So close, but too far for me to touch. Your lips swollen from our kiss. Is your pussy wet for me, B? She felt heat course through her blood blazing a circular path, searing every cell in her body as she realized she was hearing him, just as he could hear her. *The connection will strengthen, B. Your mom told me it would get stronger as our hearts became one.* Brooklyn gasped in surprise, her heart skipping a beat at the mention of her mother.

Luke told her once how grateful he was to have gotten to spend time with her mom before the accident, but at the time, she'd still been grieving and hadn't had the strength to ask him what the two of them talked about. She'd thought about asking at various times since, but the timing had never been right. *That's a lie, and you know it.* Admonishing herself, Brooklyn felt her frustration rise a split second before Luke's soothing voice drifted through her mind.

Don't be so hard on yourself, B. It's okay to be afraid, baby, but it's not okay to struggle with them alone. I want you to bring those fears to me. A shared burden divides it by more than half.

His reassurance was like a warm blanket on a cold winter night, and Brooklyn let out a breath she hadn't realized she was holding. When he crooked his finger, letting her know he wanted her to come to him, she was on her feet moving before her mind caught up with her body's response. As soon as she was within reach, he shackled her wrists with his large hands and pulled her close.

"Come. Let's walk around a bit before your brothers show up. I promised them we'd be out of the way before eleven. That gives us plenty of time to explore before we go back to the apartment." He felt her insecurity and stopped. Turning until they were face to face, Luke tilted her chin up to seal his lips over hers in a kiss that rocketed from a sweet reassurance to a fierce claiming in under five seconds. The wolf whistles from nearby broke the spell. He ended the kiss and pulled her against his chest to slow his racing heart.

"Christ in heaven. You are already stealing my sanity, and it was just a kiss." When she shuddered in his arms, he smiled.

"Don't think I don't want to play with you in the club, because I do—more than you can possibly know, but I won't compromise your dignity with your brothers by using a private room here. Even the private rooms are subject to monitoring by Dungeon Monitors, and that small window of time leaves open the chance your brothers could see or hear our scene. It's a very small chance— but an unnecessary risk." He felt her relax in his hold. Satisfied they were ready to move on, he stepped back.

"As we walk around the club, you are welcome to ask questions, but it's important you don't disrupt the scene. Keep your tone respectful and speak as unobtrusively as possible. If I can't give you a full answer right then, we'll continue the discussion later." Threading his fingers through hers, he turned and started walking toward the first scene area. "The important thing for you to remember is this is about finding out what interests you and what you are absolutely not interested in trying. I know you've researched the lifestyle enough to understand the basics, but seeing a scene is much different than reading about it."

"I appreciate you showing me around. I agree it's easier to understand the dynamics when I can see it firsthand. I was never good at figuring things out from books alone. I've always been better at practical experience than theoretical." He smiled at her analysis. That was his Brooklyn— always leading with her head. Luke would make it his mission to teach her how to let go of those tethers to reason so she could discover the freedom of submission.

Stepping close enough to the first scene for Brooklyn to be able to see the couple on stage, Luke kept her hand wrapped in his as he pulled her back against his chest, keeping his arm wrapped securely around her. He relished the physical contact, but he also knew he could monitor her body's responses better if she was pressed firmly against him. There was also the added benefit of being better able to sense any reluctance or fear, the two things he wanted to avoid at all costs.

"Watch how focused the Dom is on the woman who has put herself in his care. I'm told they have done scenes together several times before tonight, but they aren't a couple." The Dom's focus was one of the reasons he'd wanted her to see this scene. Brooklyn was incredibly insightful, so she'd quickly realize the connection between a couple would be even stronger. "He's focused on the base of her neck, monitoring every change in her pulse, no matter how small. I'd be willing to bet he could tell you exactly what her respiration rate is as well. He sees the blush spreading from her chest and is timing the strokes of his flogger to maximize her anticipation."

"I've never seen anyone bound to a St. Andrew's cross before. It's so different from what I imagined." Brooklyn's words were spoken quietly, their breathless tone going straight to his cock. At this rate, he was going to be sporting a permanent zipper tattoo along its length.

"This one was specially made for the smaller subs. Ian is very conscientious with equipment, especially since his wife is so petite. He's redesigned and re-engineered almost every apparatus in the club to suit smaller submissives.

Some of the male submissives are over a foot taller than the women—it's ridiculous to assume the equipment could be one size fits all."

Watching the sub bound to the cross tumble into subspace was an added bonus Luke hadn't expected. Brooklyn's body was practically vibrating in his arms, her desire to experience what she was seeing rolling off her in waves. Slipping his hand inside the halter top of her dress, Luke cupped her breast and groaned aloud when she arched into his touch. Nipping the sensitive area where her neck joined her shoulder, Luke felt his cock tighten even more at her full body shudder.

"See how her body reacts when she dances along the line that divides pleasure and pain? They're two sides of the same coin, but the concept is difficult to grasp until you feel it yourself." He'd been rolling the tight bud of her nipple between his fingers while he'd been speaking, punctuating the last point by squeezing the sensitive tissue between calloused fingers until she gasped in surprise.

"I can hardly wait to see your pink nipples decorated with clamps, they'll be exquisite." *I wonder if I can talk her into getting them pierced?* "I can smell your arousal, baby. It's the sweetest scent in the entire world. When we get upstairs, I'm going to tie you to the bed, so you are completely at my mercy. I'll trace every sweet fold of your pussy with my tongue, savoring the taste of your honey, imprinting it onto my soul. You'll think you're going to lose your mind, you'll unravel so many times. I won't stop until we're both completely exhausted and melting into the mattress."

Brooklyn's entire body shook violently in his embrace,

and he felt her knees weaken as she flooded his fingers with her release. Knowing she'd been able to come surrounded by people while watching a scene was beyond hot. She shook her head and turned in his arms.

"It wasn't the scene... it was you. Your words. Your touch. Those are the things that turned me on, Master." Her use of the title humbled him more than she would ever know. It seemed as though he'd waited forever to hear that word slip from between her lips, and it was worth every moment of anxiety she'd given him.

"I'm honored, B. I'm also impatient. Let's go. We'll tour the club again some other night. And I promise, the road between the mountain house and Prairie Winds will be well-traveled." He didn't wait for her to pull herself together, he shackled her wrist once again with his large hand and set a quick pace toward the secured door leading to the private apartments attached to the club.

Passing a smaller stage partially shielded from the rest of the club by large potted plants, Luke smiled at Ian's mock salute with the oversized paddle he was using on Callie. Her bare ass was a lovely shade of pink, and Luke knew the large surface area of the impact implement was spreading the blow over a wide enough surface, Ian was sending the vibration from each blow all the way to her core without causing her any real pain. Luke could hear her gasping and begging for permission to come, but he doubted Ian was going to give in easily. The man had a sadistic streak a mile wide when it came to *funishment* scenes.

Leading Brooklyn quickly down the hall, Luke knew all the time he'd spent training was for this moment. Once he'd realized he was a sexual Dominant, Luke immersed himself in learning everything he could about the lifestyle. He was lucky enough to have an uncle who worked at one of the country's top kink clubs, and Mitch Grayson never balked at answering a question, no matter how personal the inquiry. Mitch put him in touch with several Doms at various clubs around the country, allowing him to train with Dominants with different styles and specialties.

Cameron Barnes in Texas and Ian McGregor in D.C. both had reputations as strict sexual Dominants, their insistence on high protocol with their submissives was practically legendary, but Luke had been able to hear both men's inner dialogue and quickly discovered they were completely besotted by the women they considered the center of their lives. Alex and Zach Lamont at the ShadowDance Club in Colorado were both known for their adherence to protocol, but their approaches were starkly different. The same could be said for Kyle and Kent West at Prairie Winds near Austin. Both of the West brothers were demanding, but their methods were essentially polar opposites—Kyle demanded, Kent sweet-talked.

Taz Ledek at Mountain Mastery in Montana was the Dom whose style most closely matched his own. Taz's natural ability to read people wasn't as strong as Luke's gift, but it gave the other man a unique understanding of what Luke faced during scenes. Not only was it difficult to separate what a submissive was feeling from what they needed, it was often nearly impossible to shut out the rampant emotions of the other players in the room. The healing techniques Taz learned from his Lakota Grandmother and the guided meditations helped, as well as a nasty tasting potion helped still the voices when they became overwhelming.

Brooklyn cast him a curious look as he pressed his palm to the biometric reader opening the apartment door. "Who is Taz? The name sounds familiar, but I'm not sure why."

"A good friend of mine. He and his brother, Nate, own and operate Mountain Mastery in Montana. I'm looking forward to you meeting them, you may recognize their wife's pen name, Keme Meadows." He laughed out loud when her mouth dropped open. "I'll take that as a yes. You'll love her, she's very down to earth and humble about her success." Brooklyn still had a starstruck twinkle in her eyes, making Luke wonder how big a fan she really was of Taz and Nate's sweet wife.

As soon as the door closed behind them, Luke stepped back and crossed his arms over his chest. The move was the only thing keeping him from shredding the dress she was wearing as he let his gaze move slowly over her, savoring the view of every delicious inch.

"It's a beautiful dress, but unless you want it laying in tatters on the floor, you'd better take it off quickly. I want to see every inch of you."

Leaning the crutch she was still using against the wall, Brooklyn moved her fingers to the hem of the dress. Luke noticed her fingers trembled, but the sweet scent of her arousal reassured him her nervousness wasn't from fear. Lifting the dress over her head, Brooklyn exposed bare skin, inch by glorious inch until she clutched the garment in her hand, wobbling a bit as she balanced on one foot. Taking the dress from her with one hand while using the other to steady her, Luke draped the discarded dress over the back of a nearby chair.

Without giving her a chance to protest, Luke scooped her into his arms and moved quickly down the short hallway to the master bedroom. Placing her gently in the center of the large bed, he didn't waste any time securing her hands above her head. The deep blue silk scarf he used to bind her hands was a stark contrast against her skin. Luke traced his fingers along the edge of the smooth silk, wishing they'd been able to stay in the Caribbean. The warm sunshine would have restored the glow to her skin, and he knew the energy of the ocean would have helped ease the bone-weary look he saw in her eyes when she didn't think anyone was watching.

As soon as he could, Luke planned to move them both into the house in New Mexico. It's sun-drenched solarium and the mineral spring he'd lined with native rock to create a healing spa would help restore her body and spirit. All of that was going to have to wait—what wouldn't wait was the woman bound to his bed.

He'd wrapped another piece of silk around each of her slender ankles, pulling her legs wide apart, then added another binding around her injured leg to further protect her. The wound was almost healed, and he knew the hardware Dr. Monroe added wasn't going anywhere.

In some ways, she was lucky the damage required the steel screws and plates Evan had used, they would hold everything in place while her bone mended itself. What they hadn't told her yet was how soon the doctor said she could begin walking without assistance. There wasn't any reason to let her push herself more than she already was. *Hell, if she finds out she's been cleared to walk, she'll sign up for a damned marathon.*

Chapter Nineteen

B ROOKLYN WAS CONVINCED her mind was going to shatter from the pleasure building steadily in the very depths of her soul. Her pulsing core was sending bolts of fire through every cell in her body, and it was taking an inordinate amount of her concentration just to remember to breathe.

"Please..." She wasn't sure exactly what she was asking for, but her entire world was splintering as Luke's tongue traced patterns over the heated skin. Not being able to move, knowing she was his to pleasure as he saw fit felt oddly erotic. Brooklyn had always prided herself on her ability to control herself no matter what was happening around her, but letting go of her control and putting herself in Luke's capable hands felt right. The trust they'd built over the years as friends morphed seamlessly into trust as lovers, and there was a small part of her that wondered if it was too easy.

"It seems easy because you are only thinking about this moment, baby. You aren't considering the years I've waited for you to be ready. The hundreds of nights I stared silently into the darkness instead of sleeping as I lay awake wondering how I could make you mine." He'd spoken the words against her bare skin, tracing every inch until she was sure he'd never reach his goal.

"I'll get there, patience, my sweet sub. I want to make absolutely certain you are ready." He pushed the tip of his finger through the wet folds of her sex and smiled when her muscles quivered in anticipation. "You're so tight. Hell, you are going to send me over the edge into oblivion on the first thrust if I don't stretch you a bit."

Brooklyn was thrashing her head back and forth as her body responded to every word. "I want to push your control, Sir."

"Fuck me. You are playing with fire, baby. Be very careful what you wish for, my control is already hanging by a damned thread."

"I don't care, I want you. Raw need is clawing at me from the inside. I'm not sure I'll survive if I have to wait any longer."

"You will. Don't you dare come without permission, Brooklyn. I may not be able to drape your bare ass over my lap just yet, but I can still flip you over on this bed and paddle your delectable derrière until it's a fire engine red." Any other time she might be tempted to test him, but right now she wanted him to fuck her, so it wasn't in her best interest to push the issue. "Such a wise decision, baby. I plan to make you very glad you made the right choice."

Pushing his finger deeper, Luke fucked her with slow strokes of the single digit until he felt the walls of her vagina fluttering. Pulling his finger out, he gave her a couple of seconds to recover before pushing back through the rapidly swelling tissues with two fingers. Brooklyn relished the burn of her stretching tissues. Letting her head sink into the pillow, she closed her eyes so she could focus on the sensations bombarding her.

When Luke curled his fingers to press against her G-spot, Brooklyn began to pant as she fought hard to hold back the tidal wave of pleasure she felt closing in around her. It was a losing battle, but she wasn't going to surrender without a fight. She was rapidly approaching the point of no return, and for the first time since she'd learned he could hear her thoughts, she was grateful for their enhanced connection.

"Oh, I can hear you sweetheart, but I appear to have more faith in your control than you do."

She could hear the amusement in his voice, but her body was racing out of control so quickly, she couldn't concentrate on anything but frantically trying to grasp any thread of control she could. Brooklyn tried to block out all the questions flooding her mind... How many sexual partners had Luke had in the years since college? How had he learned how to light a woman's body on fire with his touch? Hell, how many women had he taken to bed, and how could she be sure she wasn't going to end up another notch in his bedpost when this was all said and done?

A snarl came from deep in Luke's throat, and she felt his frustration wash over her in a surprising burst of heat. She'd never experienced anything like the connection she felt binding her soul to his. The heat fused them together, and while she was trying to sort through the emotions, he pulled his fingers from her depths. Before she could voice her displeasure, he pushed his cock in with one thrust. The intensity of the intrusion sent fire arcing through every cell in her body in the same instant.

Luke's growled his permission to come, and those few words were all it took for her to let go and fly. Watching as stars exploded behind her eyelids, she hurtled into a brilliant nova of light as beautiful as anything Brooklyn had ever seen. The sound of Luke shouting her name as he stiffened above her brought her back to the moment. Feeling his cock swelling and jerk in her depths sent her body tumbling into another storm of pleasure. The second ride wasn't as mind-numbing, but it was every bit as intense because she'd been mentally present to enjoy his pleasure melding with her own.

Brooklyn felt Luke's hands caressing her ankles and wondered when he'd moved. She'd been so lost in the moment, she hadn't registered anything other than the lingering echoes of lightning tracing over the surface of her skin.

Knowing you were lost in the moment was the hottest thing I've ever seen, baby. I can't wait to send you deep into subspace—that place where time and reality are traded for an escape from everything bogging you down.

LUKE WATCHED AS Brooklyn's eyes took on the detached look of a woman sated, her eyelids drooping as she slipped into much-needed sleep. Kissing her forehead, he whispered the words he knew her soul needed to hear even if her mind wasn't ready.

"Mine. You belong to me just as I belong to you, sweet B. I love you, and I know in your heart you love me, too. We just need to get your head and heart on the same page."

Tucking blankets around her, Luke moved from the bed. Grabbing clothes and his phone, he stepped into the en suite bathroom just as his phone vibrated with a new message.

Mendoza onsite tomorrow. Sit-rep in Ian's office at eight a.m. My ETA is seven, make breakfast. Medical report is C-4.

Laughing at his uncle's cryptic message, Luke wondered how explosive a medical report had to be to merit Mitch flying all night across the country to deliver the news in person. Sending a quick reply, letting Mitch know the apartment was fully stocked and breakfast would be waiting, Luke settled down with his laptop and got to work. He hadn't spent any significant amount of time working since leaving for Mendoza's island estate to rescue Brooklyn, and the inattention was showing. Shaking his head at the number of emails filling his inbox, Luke wondered if it wasn't time to hire additional help. He was already planning to ask Brooklyn to work as a consultant, but he also knew Ian and several others were currently arguing about which of them was going to hire her. Luke didn't care which offer she accepted as long she could work remotely. He'd designed an office in the New Mexico house with her in mind—it was perfect for her, even including a media presentation area so she could train other retrieval agents without leaving the safety of home.

Smiling as he read the latest update from the general contractor he'd hired for the house, Luke was pleased to hear how close they were to finishing up. He knew the man and his crew had already been contacted by members of the ShadowDance and Prairie Winds teams to build or remodel their homes, and he'd recently heard Ian mention building a mountain cabin. God only knew what Ian McGregor would call a *cabin*.

The contractor would put the finishing touches on the house in the next few days, he was waiting for the final security equipment test before sealing the last wiring harnesses behind sheetrock. Luke promised to fly to Taos next week to sign off on the project so the crew could move on. He'd jokingly recommend they avoid Texas in the summer and Colorado in the winter, but he didn't have any idea where they were headed next.

He was just finishing up the last of what he'd hoped to accomplish when he noticed Brooklyn standing in the open doorway. She'd wrapped one of the bed sheets around her, so it looked like a sexy lavender toga, her hair was tousled from their earlier lovemaking, and her eyes were still bleary from sleep as she leaned against the crutch he knew she'd been using less and less when she didn't think anyone was watching.

"I woke up alone." Her simple words carried a powerful punch. Luke hadn't intended to work so long, he'd wanted to be wrapped securely around her by the time she'd awakened. Damn it, he knew she didn't sleep well, and it was something he hoped to help her with. Holding out his hand, he was pleased when she didn't hesitate to make her way to him.

"I'm sorry, baby. Time got away from me—occupational hazard." She settled on his lap without hesitation, and he smiled when she slipped her fingers under the hem of his short-sleeved shirt to caress his bicep. The cool tips of her fingers heated his skin sending a surge of electricity straight to his cock.

Knowing the mess with Mendoza would likely wrap up in the next day or two, Luke felt a wave of relief knowing they'd soon be on their way to the sanctuary he'd created in New Mexico. There was a chance he was putting all his eggs in one basket, as his grandfather used to say, but he didn't think so. He'd spent a lot of time in the mountains and felt their healing magic, so he understood how powerful the restoration could be.

Pulling the sheet tighter around Brooklyn when she shivered, Luke settled back in the oversized office chair and took a few minutes to simply enjoy the feel of Brooklyn in his arms. He'd waited years for moments like this, and it was everything he'd hoped it would be. Luke had never been one to sit quietly, but it felt remarkably right with Brooklyn in his arms.

"Mitch is flying in tonight and will be joining us for breakfast." She'd been relaxed in his arms but stiffened before shifting, so they were face to face. He cringed at the look of panic on her face.

"I still can't cook. Even if I wasn't using the crutch, I wouldn't try to make anything requiring a stove. Geez. This has disaster written all over it. Mitch knows me. Why would he come here for a meal?" By the time she finally stopped for a breath, Brooklyn was shaking like a leaf.

"Brooklyn, stop. Have you forgotten I can cook?" He watched as the fog of alarm faded, and she became focused on what he'd said. "Take a deep breath and tell me what brought this on." Her whole body seemed to sag, and he hated the feeling of defeat he felt coming off her in waves.

"I don't really know... I think I'm just tired. I knew I

was pushing myself too hard, but I wanted to finish the amulet retrieval, then I was going to quit. I wish I could tell you why it seemed so important to do the Mendoza job, but I can't. Sometimes, I think it was pride because the insurance company was so convinced it couldn't be done. Other times, I think I just had my head up my ass."

This was the Brooklyn he'd fallen in love with—the brutally honest woman who understood her own failings but didn't apologize for them. God in heaven, he loved her. He'd loved her almost from the first moment they met, and he knew he'd still be in love with her when he drew his last breath.

"Let's get another few hours of sleep. I have the feeling we're going to need it." Without waiting for her to respond, he cradled her in his arms and moved down the short hall to the master bedroom. The apartment wasn't huge, but it was as secure as any military installation he'd ever been in. Even though there were no windows, Luke was surprised how effectively Ian's design team had used daylight spectrum lighting, but right now, he appreciated the absolute darkness being deep inside the island's natural cave afforded.

"I don't know how I can still be tired when I've slept so much." Brooklyn's sleepy voice drifted through the darkness as he pulled her back against his chest. At this point, Luke knew it was her spirit's exhaustion holding her physical body hostage, but that was a discussion for another time. Right now, they both needed as much rest as possible, so they'd be ready for whatever news Mitch felt was important enough it needed to be delivered in person.

Chapter Twenty

A USTIN LET HIS gaze drift around the club and wondered why none of the submissives seemed to hold any appeal for him. Damn it all to hell, he'd flown halfway across the country to check on his sisters and hoped to find some relief from the enormous stress he'd been under. Shaking his head in frustration, Austin couldn't for the life of him figure out why none of the women who'd offered themselves to him had even made his cock stir.

Hell, the only woman who'd caught his appendage's interest lately was the new assistant he'd hired before leaving Texas. Damn it, she hadn't even started work yet, and she was distracting him. Even though there wasn't a company policy against relationships in the workplace, Austin was wise enough to know there were at least a hundred reasons he'd be a fool to act on the spark he'd felt when they'd shaken hands at the end of her interview. One touch and the scent of her arousal had wrapped itself around him like a warm blanket on a cold winter's night. It covered up the sweet smell of her perfume, and he'd had to work to keep his nostrils from flaring in recognition.

His inner wolf had fought for release as Charlotte Hays walked from the room, and now, he worried he should seriously consider firing her, so he could think straight and get some damned work done. Maybe he'd just transfer her to another department if he thought it would help, but he knew her scent would make its way to him no matter where he put her in the damned building. He'd heard of wolves following the scent of a mate for miles. Sighing to himself, he wondered if the brown-eyed beauty had any clue how far she was going to push his control.

"You look like a man with a lot on his mind." Glancing to the side, Austin was surprised to see Ian McGregor standing beside his wife and submissive. The couple had been finishing up their scene when he and Israel entered the club. Austin hadn't expected to see Ian again after he'd carried Callie into one of the private aftercare rooms.

Nodding to Callie, Austin returned his attention to Ian. "You're right, but it's nothing I'm going to be able to work out until I get back to Texas, so I'm not going to dwell on it." Ian's brow raised in question, but he didn't voice the questions Austin could see in his eyes. "I want you to know how much we appreciate everything you've done for Brooklyn." Ian's expression cleared, and his eyes sparkled in a way Austin recognized, and his chuckle confirmed the fact the man had an agenda he wasn't working very hard to conceal.

"I assure you, I'm not nearly as charitable as it may seem. I'm hoping Brooklyn will agree to help me refine a new security line I've been working on. Her input will be invaluable and being able to tell potential clients she was involved in the system's development will let me charge an astronomical price for it." Callie's eyes widened at her husband's admission, letting Austin know her sharp mind was coming back online. Turning his attention to Callie, Ian smiled. "Don't look so surprised, *Carlin*. My business wasn't built doing pro bono work."

Austin wanted to laugh out loud because he couldn't begin to count the number of times he'd said the same thing to various members of his family. He'd often wondered how they thought he'd turned his father's moderately successful business into an internationally recognized conglomerate. Ian had done the same thing although he'd started with a business teetering on the verge of collapse. His business savvy was one of the things Austin admired the most about Ian McGregor.

Ian encouraged Callie to finish the sparkling water the bartender had set in front of her a few minutes earlier, then returned his attention to Austin. "Mitch Grayson will be arriving in a few hours, so I suggest you get some rest if you aren't planning to relieve the tension I see in your expression. We'll meet in my office upstairs—it isn't as large as the meeting rooms in the resort, but it's much more secure." Pressing a kiss to Callie's forehead when she set the empty glass back on the bar, Ian helped her from the stool. Holding her close until he was sure she was steady on her feet, he linked his fingers with hers and led her to one of the secured exits.

Fighting a pang of jealousy, Austin sent up a silent prayer to the Universe for guidance. Right now, he'd settle for an answer to how to proceed with Charlotte. He wasn't sure how long he'd be able to delay the inevitable, but he knew he had to proceed with the utmost caution. Revealing his secrets to her was not only risky for him and his family, it would put his entire pack at risk.

Pushing his hands deep into his pockets, hoping to conceal the raging hard-on he always sported when thinking about his new assistant, Austin made his way to the exit leading to the island's lavish resort. The rooms Ian reserved for Austin and Israel were as good as any five-star hotel he'd ever stayed in, but damn if he didn't wish he wasn't returning there alone.

Chapter Twenty-One

M ITCH GRAYSON LEANED back in his chair, sipping the oversized mug of coffee his nephew handed him as soon as he stepped through the door. Hopefully, the thick brew would give him the jolt of caffeine he needed before the meeting in Ian's office. Mitch hadn't missed how gingerly Brooklyn lowered herself onto the chair across from him. As a Dom, he recognized the almost imperceptible wince when the back of her thighs and the cheeks of her ass came into contact with the oak seat of her chair. Before he could ask, her voice drifted through his head.

"I should have just given him the damned panties."

Mitch fought his smile and wondered for the thousandth time why going without panties was such a huge issue with most submissives. He'd seen it again and again at ShadowDance, subs so reluctant to go without underwear, they risked public punishments, and it baffled every Dom he knew.

Brooklyn's fingers wrapped nervously around a cup of tea she kept frowning down into, but this time, it wasn't her abused backside she was stewing over. Listening to her internal grumbling about the *weak-assed brew* had him struggling to hold back his amusement. When Luke turned from the stove to frown at her, Mitch finally lost the battle and laughed out loud.

"You might want to stop complaining about the tea, sweetness, or Luke's going to burn our breakfast out of spite. And after the mayo and cheese sandwich I had on the plane, I'm anxious for something with a bit more substance." At Brooklyn's confused look, he chuckled. "If I had my guess, I'd say my lovely wife was distracted by Bryant while she was making my care package. He just returned from a two-week work trip, and I should probably be impressed there was anything in the box at all."

"I'm surprised the Lamonts don't at least keep a jar of peanut butter on board for emergencies." Mitch rolled his eyes because his nephew knew perfectly well the Lamont's jet was a damned flying four-star hotel. Hell, the media room had a popcorn machine and soda fountain worthy of any mall cinema.

"I don't usually ask the crew to prepare anything because Rissa likes to make and send along my favorites. I'm going to enjoy punishing her for skipping the meat in my sandwich. It will be a nice distraction when she learns Bryant is leaving again next week." She wasn't going to be happy to learn her other husband was leaving again so soon, but he suspected she'd be much happier when she found out Bryant had decided to take a much less active role in the engineering firm he'd built from the ground up. Bryant Davis had done what none of his friends figured would ever happen—he'd decided to sell forty-nine percent of the business and retire as CEO.

"When are you going to tell her?" Mitch blinked at Luke's direct question. It always surprised him when his nephew listened in on his thinking despite the fact it had been happening since the kid learned to talk. Laughing to himself, he wondered if his expression reflected the same disbelief he regularly saw on the faces of people he read.

"I'll let Bryant tell her, and I suspect he better do so quickly because she'll see it on the internet soon if he doesn't. Once she learned how to set up alerts, nobody in her circle was safe."

"What did you find out about Mendoza?" Brooklyn blurted out the question, and from the surprise he saw in her expression, Mitch wondered if she hadn't really intended to play her hand so soon. Luke slid plates on to the table before sitting next to Brooklyn. He squeezed her hand in reassurance, and Mitch smiled because the whole thing was like watching a scene so like many that had taken place in his own home. Rissa's impetuous nature surfaced in the same way, and Mitch felt a pang of homesickness.

Giving Luke and Brooklyn a brief overview of the information he'd found between bites, Mitch suddenly realized the pair were no longer eating. Waving his fork at their plates indicating they should continue, he was surprised when Luke's apprehension rolled over him. Hell, his nephew was far more concerned about the upcoming meeting than Brooklyn seemed.

This wasn't a turn of events he would have ever anticipated since Luke was well acquainted with every member of the team Ian had pulled together. Mitch hoped Luke would feel more settled after the meeting, but putting himself in his nephew's shoes—he wasn't sure he'd feel comfortable until Mendoza was dealt with.

Smiling to himself, Mitch wondered what Israel Adler

was going to say when the sub he'd flogged into sub-space before carrying her into a private room where they' spent most of the night turned out to be the internationally acclaimed psychologist and criminal profiler Ian brought in as a consultant. When Luke's lips twitched, Mitch knew he'd heard his thoughts.

Ian and Mitch were the only ones who knew Dr. Alex Drummond—whose name was listed on the meeting agenda the team had already received—was actually Dr. Alexandria Drummond. Her reputation as a criminologist was well known—she'd worked for all the major alphabet agencies and written several authoritative books on profiling. What wasn't as widely known was the buxom beauty was a sexual submissive. Since Mitch had dealt with Brooklyn's abrasive younger brother before, he wondered how quickly Dr. Drummond would hand Israel Adler his balls if he assumed her sweet, docile, submissive side could be found outside the bedroom.

Luke was staring at him, his expression a mix of amusement and horror. *Don't worry. Hell, I know people who would pay good money for admission to this show.*

BROOKLYN WASN'T SURE what had taken place at breakfast, but it had been clear Luke and his uncle were communicating without speaking. She'd tried to decide whether to be amused or annoyed but had finally decided to focus on Luke, only to be disappointed when she hadn't been able to catch any of his thoughts. Trying again as he'd held her hand walking the short distance to Ian's office, she finally admitted defeat because she hadn't heard a damned thing.

"Don't worry, B, I've just had more practice blocking than most people. Just be sure you sit where you can keep your eyes on Israel—he's in for a big surprise." Luke's words didn't make sense, but she'd learned a long time ago he didn't say anything without a reason, and in all the years she'd known him, he'd rarely been wrong about anything.

Ian welcomed everyone before inviting Phoenix Morgan and Abby Garrett to explain what they'd discovered while examining the amulet. Brooklyn was relieved to learn they'd managed to open the back compartment but disappointed when it was revealed, so far, no one had been able to decode the inscription. Not everyone who'd worked on the ancient piece of jewelry was convinced it held the answer to one of Christianity's most enduring mysteries, but no one was ruling out the possibility.

When the room finally settled, Mitch moved to stand beside Ian. Thinking back on the call he'd gotten, Mitch smiled to himself. One of the joys of using the Lamonts' private jet was being able to leave as soon as you arrived at the airport. Mitch had been so anxious to share what he'd learned, he'd driven through the gates of the private side of the airport two hours early. After a quick adjustment to the flight plan, they'd taken off. A strong tailwind meant he'd arrived at the island close to the time he'd expected to leave Denver—the extra time had given him an opportunity to look at the amulet himself.

Mitch appreciated Ian letting him use one of the smaller offices to spend a few minutes quietly tapping into the power of the amulet. He wasn't ordinarily particularly good with inanimate objects, but he'd welcomed the chance to try. Luke had opted to forego reading the ancient bauble, preferring to focus his attention on Brooklyn's safety—something Mitch understood completely.

Having heard gifted friends swear the ancient Egyptians found a way to infuse their creations with an energy so powerful, it could speak to a soul centuries later had piqued Mitch's interest and made him anxious to try connecting with the mysterious power. He hadn't been disappointed.

From the moment he'd picked it up, the amulet had practically vibrated in his hands, the energy so powerful, he'd worried he might drop it. The vision that appeared in front of him was so realistic, he'd found himself reaching out to touch people walking by, only to have his hand pass through the image in a swirl of color. Standing in front of his friends and colleagues, attempting to explain the strangest experience of his life wasn't something Mitch could have ever anticipated.

"Personally, I don't think the amulet's *real* message is about the ark even though the craftsmen who made it had most certainly heard the stories about the powerful religious artifact. The message I received from the amulet was a warning of the dangers of unrest in what we now call the Middle East. The ancients foresaw the years of war and strife. Oddly enough, they made some amazingly accurate predictions about the ripple effects of religious battles and another exodus from the *center of humanity* as they referred to the region."

The only person in the room who knew Mitch wasn't being entirely transparent was Luke, and he wisely kept his reservations to himself. Mitch hadn't lied—the real message had been a warning, but it hadn't been the only message. Some secrets were best left alone. If the Ark's location was revealed, the battle its discovery would create would far out weight any problems it would solve.

Chapter Twenty-Two

BROOKLYN STARED OUT the window of Ian's office as members of the team tasked with protecting her chatted at the back of the room. Most of the team had already been sent to their posts, others were finalizing details in military speak she'd grown tired of decoding. Leaning on the crutch she'd come to hate, Brooklyn felt her brother's arm wrap around her shoulders.

"Well, that was enlightening." Israel's tone was sharper than usual, and she'd felt a pang of sympathy for him when Alex Drummond stepped into the room.

"I don't imagine this will be listed as one of the year's highlights in your Christmas letter." She knew he wouldn't miss the double meaning since he'd sent his siblings a generic letter and skipped the family holiday gathering last year. Satisfied she'd hit her mark when he winced, she shook her head. "Don't do that again, Is, we deserve better than some damned photocopied letter I suspect your secretary wrote."

"Yeah, you do. For what it's worth, I'm sorry. I tried to spare everyone my dark mood and ended up spreading the gloom without even being there." Brooklyn understood the irony, but she wasn't willing to let him completely off the hook.

"Sharing a burden isn't spreading it, little brother." Warm hands cupped her shoulders before she could finish sharing Luke's wisdom.

"I'm glad you were listening, B." The gentle squeeze he gave her tense muscles made her knees weaken. "Come. You need to do the stretches Dr. Monroe outlined before spending some time in the whirlpool." She knew Luke was right, but her leg was already throbbing, and she wasn't looking forward to the torture routine London's nemesis assigned. Luke chuckled and pulled her back against his chest, his warmth and strength infusing her with energy. Looking down at her, Luke grinned. "Don't be fooled by London and Dr. Monroe's bickering—it's nothing more than foreplay."

Israel's eyes widened, but he didn't give voice to the questions she could see dancing in their dark depths. Shuffling on the damned crutch she hated so much, Brooklyn moved until she could lean her cheek against her brother's chest and sighed.

"Please be careful tonight. I know this sort of thing is what you do every day, but that doesn't mean I'm not going to worry about you." The kiss he pressed against her hair was sweetly familiar... of all her brothers, Israel reminded her the most of their father, and the similarities seemed more pronounced with each passing year.

Brooklyn found a strange comfort knowing their dad had left behind such an enduring legacy, but the knowledge also reminded her of all they'd lost. When she was finally ready to leave, Luke lifted her into his arms, accepted the crutch from Israel's outstretched hand, and moved quickly down the hall. She could feel the need pulsing from him and wished he'd forget about the therapy and find a horizontal surface where they could fuck each other until all the tension dissipated into a fine mist. The growl deep in his chest made her look up into his darkening green eyes.

"Be careful what you wish for, baby. I'm not above making your hot fantasy a reality, and I doubt that's a scene you want your brothers walking up on." He was right… maybe. Her head knew they should wait until they were back in the apartment, but her body was screaming *Now!* so loud, she could barely hear him. "When we return to the apartment, I'll strip you naked before you can blink and have you on every available surface—horizontal and vertical—between the door and the bed."

He set her on a low stool near the exercise mat, putting her at eye level with his straining erection, and she unconsciously licked her lips. It was easy to see the outline of his cock pressing incessantly against his zipper, and she wondered how he would free himself with doing bodily harm. Damn, she hoped he didn't injure what was quickly becoming her favorite toy.

"Christ Almighty, baby, you are going to be the death of me."

AFTER PUSHING HER to stretch her taut muscles, Luke picked Brooklyn up once again and made his way through the locker room door, chuckling when she gasped. She buried her face against the side of his neck, trying to shield her eyes, but he could have saved her the trouble. The club wasn't open yet, and the bartender had been instructed to put up a sign warning away any staff already onsite.

Setting Brooklyn on one of the long wooden benches, Luke made certain she'd regained her equilibrium before moving to the large spa's control panel. Dimming the lights and closing the sliding doors surrounding the area, Luke turned his attention to the woman watching him from beneath lush lashes. Brooklyn's eyes were already half-lidded with arousal, a light flush spreading slowly over her exposed upper chest. Damn, he loved the lowcut blouses she favored, the glimpses of lace they afforded had fueled his fantasies for years.

"Strip, baby, or I'm going to shred another pretty outfit." He smiled when she huffed in exasperation. He'd already torn one of the shirts Ian had delivered when she'd ignored his warning to remove it, so she knew full well what would happen to this one. It was a good thing he'd already sent movers to her apartment in New York City. The contents had already been packed and sent to New Mexico. Hell, at least he knew she'd have some clothing when she arrived because if she wasn't careful, she'd be traveling in nothing but a sheet wrapped around her delectable body. Although the idea held a certain appeal, he needed to stop leaving her clothing in tatters on the floor— at least for now.

Callie and Catalina had gone to a lot of trouble to make certain Brooklyn had a nice wardrobe, but he'd heard her muttering about how quickly the contents of the closet would dwindle if he didn't knock it off. Smiling to himself at the thought, he chuckled when she rolled her eyes as she folded the dress and set it aside.

"I know we've both made good money over the years, but it seems wasteful to pull things apart by the seams. Maybe I should start buying granny panties, they seem like they're built to withstand almost anything." Luke wasn't sure what granny panties were, and it didn't sound like anything he was interested in investigating. Besides, she would rarely need panties of any sort.

"Baby, someday, when I'm feeling particularly brave, I'll Google *granny panties*, but I'm already fairly certain they aren't anything I'm interested in seeing you wear." Her cheeks turned a beautiful shade of pink, and he chuckled to himself, knowing he could still make her blush. "As a matter of fact, it's probably best if I take over the duty of shopping for your lingerie." Luke and Brooklyn had been friends for years, so there was no doubt she would know exactly what he was thinking.

"It's not as if the added responsibility is going to be a burden." Hell, just thinking about picking out sexy bras and crotchless panties was making his erection swell in response. And if you added corsets to the mix, his body threatened an all-out mutiny if he didn't sink into her tight pussy soon. "Are you on birth control, baby?" He could see by the way her eyes widened, his question surprised her, but she quickly nodded.

"Perfect. I have test results for you, and I want to feel your pussy clenching around me without anything separating us." He threw his clothes onto the entry table and heard her giggle when most of them slid to the floor in a haphazard pile that was a perfect reflection of his frantic effort to get naked. With his hands cupping her shoulders, Luke walked Brooklyn backward two steps until her bare back was pressed against the wall.

"What are you going to do? I thought you were in a hurry to find a bed." The breathless sound of her voice was one of the sexiest things he'd ever heard. Damn, he loved her with everything he was.

"I don't want to wait, and now that I know I don't need protection, I intend to make use of any surface available—I want to fuck you until I'm barely able to carry you to bed. I've already got everything set up. As soon as Mendoza's threat to you is neutralized, we're heading to Taos. I want you to rest surrounded by the colorful and enhanced mountains of New Mexico."

There was more—so much more, but he was tired of chatting. Gripping her shoulders, Luke lifted Brooklyn, sliding her up the wall far enough, he knew her feet were no longer touching the floor. Her quick inhalation told him he'd surprised her, and he groaned when she instinctively wrapped her slender legs around his waist.

"Oh, God. I want you so much it scares me." *And you could make me lose myself so easily.*

Luke knew one of Brooklyn's greatest fears had always been losing herself in whoever she fell in love with. She couldn't remember her mother ever having an interest outside her husband and children, and B had never been able to see herself in a similar role. Over the years, Luke had often wondered if her sisters didn't harbor similar fears. Hell, for all he knew, their fears were a subconscious reflection of their mother's insistence they all become successful in their own right before marrying.

In hindsight, Luke often wondered if their mom hadn't sensed she and Matthew wouldn't be there to help their children as adults, so Season had pushed them all—particularly the girls—to become successful in their own right, reminding them how important it was they could take care of themselves. Returning his attention to the naked woman wrapped around him like a vine, Luke trailed kisses from the top of her shoulder up the side of her neck, then nipped the lobe of her ear. The small edge of pain made her melt against him, and he felt her arousal wash over the throbbing head of his cock. Christ in heaven, if he didn't get inside her now, he was going to explode.

"Sink down on my cock, baby. I can smell your sweet honey, so I know you're more than ready to take me." Sealing his lips over hers, Luke plundered her mouth while she slipped her slender fingers between them wrapping the warm digits around his steely length. Whispering against her lips, he fought to string together words that didn't make him sound like a babbling fool.

"Fuck, baby. The touch of your fingers is almost enough to push me over the edge." She pulled back until her dark eyes met his, and he was shocked to see the heat and desire flaming in their depts.

"I want to taste you." His head fell back as the picture of her lips wrapped around his cock flashed through his mind. Fucking hell, he'd fantasized about her kneeling in front of him while he pushed himself down her throat so many times, it was burned into his psyche.

"Later, baby. Right now, all I can think about is fucking you with nothing between us. I want to see my seed trailing down your inner thighs when we step into the shower." He didn't know how to be any more transparent. There was a part of him that would probably beat his chest like a damned Neanderthal at the sight.

Pushing through her slick folds felt like sliding through wet silk. He didn't stop his upward thrust until the tip of his cock was pressed against her cervix. "Fuck me, baby, you are already rippling around me."

"More." It was the only word she managed to speak out loud, but Luke could hear her mind scrambling to express what she couldn't put into words. The only word she managed to push past her kiss-swollen lips was like gas hitting a flame. "Harder."

"I'll always give you what you need, B. Always." Fucking her with long, pounding strokes, Luke varied the timing of his thrusts, knowing it would keep Brooklyn on the cusp for as long as possible. The muscles lining the walls of her vagina flexed, and Luke groaned. "Christ, baby, you feel amazing. Pushing my bare cock into your heat is the closest thing to heaven on earth. The sensations are so much more intense, I love making love to you without anything between us." Several thrusts later Luke knew he wasn't going to last, and he was determined Brooklyn was going over first. Reaching between them, he rolled a nipple between his fingers and squeezed. "Come for me, B."

Brooklyn's response was immediate and almost took him to his knees. Her vaginal muscles tightened around him like a vise, and her honey flowed around him like hot syrup. Feeling her let go, knowing she felt safe enough to surrender to the pleasure while pressed against the wall of an unfamiliar space was enormously gratifying. Luke wasn't arrogant enough to think he'd won the war, but he planned to enjoy this small victory.

"You take my breath away, baby."

"Holy hell, you turned me into a limp rag. I hope that shower has a bench or a chair in it because I don't think either one of my legs will hold me up." Luke smiled down at her as he shifted her into his arms.

"You fried my brain, but I think I can get us both as far as the shower." *Maybe.* By the time Luke managed to turn on the shower and set out towels, Brooklyn was steady enough to stand on her own. Looking down where his seed coated the inside of her thighs made him want to beat his chest.

"Have you always been a caveman? How did I miss such an obnoxious trait?" Brooklyn's teasing tone made him smile. Knowing their connection had grown strong enough for her to hear him in unguarded moments was damned satisfying.

"Just because you chose to ignore the signs doesn't mean they weren't there. I've always been a caveman where you were concerned." And it was true, he'd always been protective to the point, he'd worried at times he might frighten her away. Refocusing his attention on finishing up their showers, he was pleased to see Brooklyn using her leg more after the intense therapy session she'd just endured. It was important she was as mobile as possible tonight—with Mendoza, the whole evening could go to hell in a heartbeat.

After he'd finally settled Brooklyn in the spa, Luke opened his mind to see if he could connect with Mendoza. Ian had ferried a therapist from D.C. to work with Brooklyn, and their time on the mat of the club's gym had given Luke a chance to catch up on the messages he'd known were lighting up his damned phone like a Christmas tree.

Reading that Mendoza was already onsite had been unsettling, and he knew he wouldn't be able to keep the information from Brooklyn for long.

"Why don't you just spit it out? It's wearing me out trying to figure out what you're worried about telling me, and it's distracting you enough you haven't noticed my foot stroking your leg."

Son of a bitch. How far up his ass was his head? His face must have shown his surprise, and before he had a chance to respond, she burst into a fit of giggles. He sat across from her, staring through the white ribbons of steam floating up from the hot water bubbling around them and couldn't take his eyes off her. The beautiful tinkling sound of Brooklyn's laughter had always made his heart skip a beat.

"WHO IS THAT man, Daddy?" Jace Garrett smiled down into the dark eyes of his daughter and felt a familiar wave of déjà vu roll over him. His young daughter might be named after him, but she looked so much like her Aunt Abby, it never ceased to take his breath away. Looking back at the monitor, he watched Emilio Mendoza saunter off the ferry, looking like he owned the place.

"He thinks he's all that and a bag of chips, doesn't he?" Her little chin lifted as she spoke, and he had to fight the urge to ask what she and Aunt Abby had done yesterday afternoon because there was no doubt in his mind they'd spent time together. With her sweet mama finishing up a screenplay, she'd have been happy to have Abby take Jacey off her hands for a few hours. He and Gage had been busy getting everything set up for Mendoza's arrival, so Holly had asked his sister to take Jacey for a few hours in hopes of finding a little peace and quiet.

Heaven knows, Jacey wouldn't be content to play with any of the other children on the island. Jace didn't think their pint-sized genius had played with other kids since she and Ian's daughter, Carlie announced they planned to set up a lab like Aunt Abby's so they could "blow up stuff." Jace wasn't sure he'd ever seen faces as pale as Holly's and Callie's when they'd come to Ian's office to report what they'd overheard. The two mothers had been much more rattled than any of the fathers, but they'd been wise enough to keep their lack of concern to themselves.

"What else do you notice about him, sweetheart?" Jace's sister's mini-me might look like a carbon copy of Abby Garrett, but she'd inherited her Daddy Gage's intuition when it came to observing people.

"I think he is looking for somebody, but he's trying to be a sneaky snake."

Sighing to himself when he heard another of his sister's favorite expressions, Jace made a mental note to find out how much longer his sister would be on the island. Watching Mendoza make his way to the cart that would take him to the resort, Jace had to agree with his daughter—the man was trying very hard to hide the fact he appeared to be casing the area.

"Is he here for the surprise party? Aunt Abby said there was going to be a party with surprises tonight at Uncle Ian's club, that's why Carlie and I are staying with her nanny." Jace chuckled to himself at her reference to Ian as her uncle because the title pleased Jace's best friend more than anyone knew.

"Did Abby also remind you the lab is off-limits unless she or Ian is with you?" Jace sent up a silent prayer, hoping neither of the girls had found a way to skirt the security system yet. *It's only a matter of time.*

"Yeah, she made a big deal about it because Daddy Gage was watching." Jace had to bite back his laughter because he could just imagine how dramatic his sister had made the warning. She'd have found Gage's scrutiny amusing, to say the least. "Uncle Ian said we get to stay in Nanny Grace's apartment, he already ordered all our favorite foods, so we don't even have to leave for snacks. As soon as Brooklyn gets better, she's going to show us how to scale the sides of walls." She must have felt him tense because she quickly added, "In case we're ever trapped in a burning building, you know."

Oh yeah, he knew alright, and he planned to make certain Luke whisked Brooklyn off to New Mexico as soon as this was resolved. *Damn, as if the girls aren't already a handful, we damned well don't need to add cat burglar to their resumes.*

Chapter Twenty-Three

B ROOKLYN WAS TIRED and frustrated. The air around them was filled with a strange energy she usually associated with a coming storm. Listening closely, she wanted to stomp her foot in annoyance. *Christ in heaven, who can hear themselves think with the music so loud?* Shifting on her feet nervously, Brooklyn wondered if the rumble she'd heard was thunder or the pounding beat of the music.

Standing at the back of Club Isola's large main room, Brooklyn focused on the interaction across the room where Ian McGregor, Abby Garrett, and Phoenix Morgan enthusiastically showed the fake amulet to the small crowd gathered around them. She wasn't sure how they'd managed it, but the "artifact" Abby held cradled so carefully in her hands looked so incredibly authentic, Brooklyn doubted many people would be able to tell it was fake.

Earlier this evening, after she'd rested for several hours, Brooklyn finally convinced Luke to let her join the team gathered in Ian's office. She was still flummoxed at how quickly they'd managed to create a replica so real, she'd been hard pressed to pick out the real amulet. Knowing the one Abby was currently gushing over was loaded with electronic gadgetry gave Brooklyn a sense of safety she hoped wasn't misplaced.

"You'll be fine as long as you stay where the team can see you at all times. You're as wired for sight and sound as we can make you." *There's a damned fact. Dr. Growly turns me into an erector set, then Ian and his merry band of geniuses turn me into a walking, talking antenna.* Luke's snort of laughter made her blush. Damn, was she ever going to get used to him listening in on her thoughts? *"Think of me as an imaginary friend you don't have to explain anything to."* His words rolled around in her mind, and even though she couldn't explain why, they eased some of her concerns.

"Have you been watching Mitch? He maneuvers into position to read Mendoza and gets cut off at the pass every time. It seems Mr. Mendoza has done his homework." Mitch's gift wasn't a closely guarded secret like Luke's had always been.

"Can you read him?"

"I'm catching bits and pieces, but there are so many people between us, I'm having trouble separating out the voices." Once he opened himself up, he was subject to a barrage of information and energy. If he was going to help Mitch, he needed to be a lot closer to Mendoza, but he wasn't sure how Brooklyn would feel about being left on her own. He knew as soon as the thoughts went through his mind she'd heard him because she turned her attention to him as her eyes narrowed.

"You have to be fucking kidding me. I don't need a babysitter, Luke. I took care of myself for a very long time. I will survive hanging out by myself for a few minutes, and I'm the one who's going to benefit by having this mess cleared up." *Yeah, me and all the other people wasting time and money on this foolishness.* Luke frowned and shook his head.

"We aren't wasting time or money, B. Looking out after friends and family is what people do." He must have seen the regret in her eyes because he shook his head and continued. "Don't go there, baby. I don't want you to feel guilty. Since it's obviously not a problem for you to wait here, I'm going to move closer and see what I can find out." His quick glance toward where Mendoza stood looking on as Abby explained what they'd "discovered" was all it took for Brooklyn to know how much Luke wanted to help.

As relieved as she was to have Luke moving closer to help Mitch, with each step he took, she felt their connection fray a little more at the edges. It was unnerving after having him close for so long. *We'll be going to the mountain cabin soon, and it'll be just the two of us forever.* The relief she felt when his voice whispered in her mind sent a wave of warmth through her making her smile.

MOVING CLOSER TO Emilio Mendoza was like stepping into a dark void. Luke fought back the urge to shiver at the cold maleficent energy surrounding the other man. Mitch met his gaze, and Luke knew his uncle understood what had caused his hesitance. Mendoza was far more dangerous than any of them had anticipated, making Luke wish he'd given Brooklyn one last warning about not leaving without taking someone with her.

Moving within a few feet of Mendoza, Luke had to focus solely on his thoughts while trying to set aside the vacuum surrounding him. It was an emptiness Luke could barely tolerate and had no idea how to describe. One of his college professors had insisted Hell wasn't filled with fire and brimstone, rather it was a place of abject emptiness. At the time, Luke hadn't fully understood how *nothingness* could be Hell, but the concept was suddenly perfectly clear.

The first thing Luke noticed was Mendoza's self-talk sounded more like that of an angry teenager than an adult operating their own business. After what they'd learned from Dr. Drummond, he shouldn't have been surprised the man appeared to be speaking to someone no one else could see, but he was shocked to realize Mendoza was taking direction from the delusion. Listening closely, Luke was so focused on Mendoza, he didn't sense Brooklyn's rising alarm.

CARLIE LOOKED UP from her tablet and grinned when Jacey walked in the room. "I have the most scathingly brilliant idea. Wait until you hear."

"You watched that Haley Mills movie, again didn't you? I can always tell." Jacey loved to tease her friend about her love for old movies, but the truth was she enjoyed them as much as Carlie. "Okay, tell me what sort of trouble we're going to get into tonight."

"Dad said we could do experiments as long as we used household items, and I wanted to make balloon bombs, but I used up all the ones I had, trying to find things that would be fun to watch explode on the beach." Jacey wondered if they were going to be able to talk Nanny Grace into letting them throw balloons off the balcony of her apartment but decided to let Carlie worry about that detail.

In Jacey's opinion, her friend rarely had any trouble dealing with most adults, including her nanny. Carlie had her dad wrapped around her little finger, but her mom was a different story. Callie McGregor was what Jacey's mom called a *force to be reckoned with* and usually the one to see through her schemes. Jacey wasn't sure throwing balloons off the balcony sounded very exciting, but her Aunt Abby kept telling her to get her nose out of her books and live a little, so decided to keep her doubts to herself.

"Since I used up all my balloons testing the splat-factor, I raided my mom's bedside table." Jacey rolled her eyes because she already knew where her friend was headed. Just because she was still in grade school didn't mean she didn't know what condoms were. Carlie had told her all about them last summer when they'd found a box under the boat dock. Now that she thought about it, the two of them had enjoyed the water balloon fight they'd had thanks to a guest's carelessness.

Grinning at Carlie, Jacey asked, "Are you prepared to be a big sister, again?"

"Don't be a drama queen. My dad is already convinced I'm training my little brother to be a terrorist." Carlie rolled her eyes, but it was easy to see she hadn't taken the accusation to heart. "I have news for everybody, little brother is a pacifist. He'll end up living in a lab, wear pastel colored shirts with pocket protectors, and marry a girl with glasses so thick, they look like they were cut them from the bottom of a soda bottle."

Jacey giggled at her friend's observation because it was hard enough to imagine her sweet little brother as an adult, but it was even harder to imagine Callie letting him wear pastel colored shirts since she practically melted into a puddle whenever Uncle Ian walked in wearing his usual black, button-up shirt.

"Good grief, will you focus already? We have to get these things filled with green Jell-O and oatmeal before Nanny Grace figures out they aren't balloons and we didn't use ice water. I Googled what to use besides water and got lots of suggestions, but I think combining these has the most potential. The sticky Jell-O will help the oatmeal dry faster, so it sets up like concrete."

"Please tell me you put some of your glow in the dark glitter in the Jell-O." Jacey was starting to see where this plan had real potential, especially if things at the party got out of hand. Maybe they'd end up catching a bad guy… that would definitely give them bragging rights when they went back to school in a couple of weeks.

EMILIO WATCHED IN his peripheral vision as his associate pulled Brooklyn Adler back into the shadows. With that part of this mission completed, he turned his attention to the small, locked case he knew contained the amulet. It had been years since he'd stolen anything, but he was confident he'd be able to get as far as the boat before anyone noticed it was missing. By the time they tracked him to the lesser used dock in front of the resort, he'd be well on his way. No doubt they'd expect him to return to his home, but he had no intention of getting caught, so he was circling to the south before returning to a marina a few miles south of D.C.

Stealthily pushing the velvet pouch containing the amulet deep in his pocket, Emilio set the locked box back in place before any of the people milling around noticed. He appreciated his mother reminding him that he had once been very good at picking locks. Often her reminders sounded a lot like criticism, but he tried to remain patient with her—dealing with her could drive a man stark raving mad when she was in one of her moods.

Slipping out an exit he'd chosen earlier, he was grateful for the foliage shielding its door from the security cameras on the outside of the club. He was surprised the Club security team had overlooked the overgrowth, but who was he to look a gift horse in the mouth? The coming storm was also going to play in his favor. Heavy, oppressive air suppressed the sound of his footfalls, and except for the intermittent flashes of lightning, the heavy cloud cover kept the night totally dark.

After walking several yards toward the dock closest to the club, Emilio darted into the heavy shrubbery and quickly reversed directions. Filled with a renewed sense of purpose, he made his way through the heavy brush, determined to find the woman who'd set this nonsense in motion. He'd secured the amulet and looked forward to dealing with Brooklyn Adler—nothing was going to stand in his way.

Chapter Twenty-Four

B ROOKLYN'S FEET WERE barely brushing the cobblestone walk which meant she couldn't get any traction to stop the asshat dragging her away from Club Isola. She could see the resort ahead of them and instinctively knew allowing him to drag her to the dock meant she'd virtually have no way to escape. The man wasn't much taller than she was, but Brooklyn sensed she was no match for him in a fight, and God knew, she wouldn't be able to outrun him.

Trying to grab a low-hanging branch as they walked out of the heavily wooded area behind the club earned her a fist to the side of her face. Dammit, her ears were ringing, and there were black dots dancing in front of her eyes. *You just signed your death warrant when Luke and my brothers find out you hit me, you bastard. I'm going to enjoy watching them take your ass apart.*

Straining to keep from slipping into the bliss of unconsciousness, Brooklyn searched the resort for anyone she might enlist as help. The son of a bitch holding her had wrapped his arm around her waist, so it looked like he was helping rather than forcing her. Brooklyn knew other guests would assume they shared an intense scene at the club, so it was doubtful anyone would intervene. *Like I would ever scene with Mr. Stinky. Damn, don't they sell deodorant in your cave?*

Glancing up, Brooklyn felt her eyes widen at what appeared to be someone looking her direction with a pair of pink binoculars. *Great, now I'm hallucinating. Mr. Stinky must have hit me harder than I thought.* Her head hurt so bad, Brooklyn was almost afraid to try to connect with Luke, but she knew it was her only chance. As soon as she opened her mind, his warmth stilled her rising panic.

"Open your mind to me, Brooklyn. Let me see what you see, it will help us find you."

"THAT MAN JUST hit Brooklyn. Did you see that? Boy, our dads will be mad when they hear about this. Maybe Nanny Grace should call them." Jacey quickly realized Carlie was grabbing the sling-shot her mom had hidden a few weeks ago when she'd been caught shooting rocks at passing boats. "Hey, where did you find that?"

"Hiding spot number six—for someone as smart as my mom, she isn't very good at hiding stuff. I mean, come on, you're not even trying when you use the same numerical pattern when choosing a hiding place. Even numbers for two rounds and then odds for two rounds." Carlie hadn't stopped moving as she'd answered, and before Jacey realized what was happening, her partner in crime was launching the green gel-oatmeal filled condoms at the couple moving quickly toward them.

The first one splattered a few feet in front of the man who'd hit Brooklyn, causing him to curse so loud, Jacey heard every word. "Boy, his mom should have washed his mouth out with soap." Grabbing more *ammunition*, she handed the colorful condoms to Carlie. "Hit him right in the face like he did Brooklyn. He's a jerk, men aren't supposed to hit women."

"My mom says women aren't supposed to hit men either, but I think we'll get a pass on this one since he started it." Jacey wanted to laugh at her friend because she figured they were going to be in a lot more trouble for the condom grenades than they were for hitting the man carrying Brooklyn away.

The next green oatmeal bomb hit the man in the crotch making him drop his hold on Brooklyn. She staggered but finally took a few steps to the side.

"Good, she's out of range. Hand me some more, quick." Jacey watched as Carlie launched the condoms as fast as she could hand them over. The man staggered and finally fell to his knees as he was pelted with shot after shot. A few seconds later, a second man ran out of the trees and hurtled himself in Brooklyn's direction. Before he could reach her, one of Carlie's oatmeal missiles hit him in the chest and another right between his eyes. Brooklyn stood to the side, hanging onto one of the garden statues Carlie's mom called landscaping, her mouth gaping open in surprise before she started laughing and cheering them on.

Jacey and Carlie laughed as the men struggled to their feet, the oatmeal hardening so fast, they turned into creepy green statues just like Google said they would. Jacey was relieved to see people surround the men because they only had one *balloon* left, and it was frightening to think about what else Carlie might have decided to use for ammo.

"I see you've mastered trajectory, Carlie." Nanny Grace's amused voice sounded from behind them. When she and Carlie spun around to face the elderly woman, all they saw was amusement dancing in her blue eyes. "Before the pandemonium makes its way to us, I want to take a moment to suggest the two of you level with your parents. I suspect this may be the only time you'll get a free pass on so many transgressions. Hopefully, your grace will extend to me since it's painfully obvious I should have been watching you a lot closer." She winked at them, then laughed, "I agreed to water and food coloring, not lime green oatmeal. I swear you two never cease to amaze me."

LUKE BURST THROUGH the foliage in desperate search of Brooklyn, knowing the coming storm was likely making a horrible experience even more traumatic. Rushing from the surrounding shrubbery, he was stunned to find her only a few steps to his right. He literally saw red when he noticed tears streaming from her swollen eye and the dark bruise on her cheek. Barely managing to hold back his anger, it was only when he wrapped her in his arms, he felt amusement pouring from her rather than fear.

"You've scared at least a decade off my life, B, would you mind telling me what's so damned funny?" *And why the hell you left without reaching out to me?* The first image he'd gotten from her had been of what looked like green brain matter splattered on a slate walkway, and he'd almost dropped to his knees as fear for her swamped him. It was only after he'd taken a breath and realized it was *green*, not red, he'd been able to pull in a deep breath.

"The girls saved me. Can you believe it? I was rescued by two elementary school girls with condoms filled with lime-green goo."

Luke shook his head and smiled, but he couldn't bring himself to let her go because he knew there was an adrenaline crash in her near future. The thought had no sooner skittered through his mind, she started to shake so violently, he picked her up in his arms before she collapsed.

The chaos around them was broken up with laughter as team members realized they might have to chisel the perps out of a mixture that was turning out to be almost as strong as concrete even though it smelled a whole lot sweeter. Ian stepped up beside them, and Luke could hear his internal laughter as he took in the scene.

"Christ, this has Carlie's name written all over it. I'm not sure I even want to ask how she and Jacey managed to fill what looks suspiciously like condoms with—good God, is that Jell-O? Fuck me, is that oatmeal?" Ian's voice was rising in pitch, but Luke wanted to laugh at the pride he could feel coming off the man in waves.

"Gage is in the control center and said he just checked the girls' search histories and confirmed it's probably oatmeal." Luke wasn't sure when Jace had joined them, but he found himself smiling at the amusement lacing the man's voice. "Nanny Grace called me a moment ago, asking me to remember the girls saved the day when we talk to them." This time he didn't try to hold back his laughter.

"You know Callie and Holly are going to have a fit. I don't even want to think about how I'm going to tell her our daughter has turned into a mad scientist." Ian's words seemed to bring Brooklyn back to the moment because she pushed out of his hold and limped the few steps to face Ian and Jace.

"If it wasn't for those two heroines, I'd be on a damned boat to nowhere. We all know I'd have never gotten out of that alive. Mr. Stinky over there," she waved her arm in the direction of the larger green statue, "told me Emilio Mendoza planned to make an example of me."

"Mr. Stinky?" Jace hadn't even tried to hold back his chuckle.

"Yes. Your men will find out soon enough, under all the sweet lime scent is a man who needs to be introduced to a stick of deodorant." Brooklyn's ability to bounce back from what he knew had been a terrifying few minutes amazed him.

CATALINA LEANED AGAINST a moss-covered tree, trying to let her heart catch up with what she was seeing a few feet ahead of her. For the first time in her life, she was so overwhelmed with relief, she couldn't move. She'd been following Mendoza, taking the five o'clock position when he'd suddenly changed directions. The son of a bitch would have run into her if Cooper hadn't pulled her behind a large pine tree.

When she'd opened her mouth to protest, he'd sealed his lips against hers, silencing her in a way only Cooper Hicks could. What is it about the damned man she couldn't resist? It was infuriating and exciting all at once, but now that they'd made their way to where all seemed to have broken loose and she could see her sister was alright, Cat felt like a puppet whose strings had been cut.

"You okay, Princess?" Cooper's warm breath brushed the shell of her ear, and Cat couldn't hold back the shiver that moved up her spine. He encircled her with one arm, brushing the underside of her unbound breasts, reminding her how little she was wearing. Damn, how had she let them talk her into wearing something so skimpy when she was supposed to be working.

Shaking her head in an attempt to move past the desire igniting in her, Cat watched as men from several law enforcement divisions tried to maneuver Mendoza's and his stooge's arms behind their backs.

"What's all over them? It looks like they tried to make themselves look like concrete statues... really sticky, lime statues." She's lost her communication device in the wooded area behind the club and had been out of the loop since.

"It seems Carlie McGregor and Jacey Garrett have saved the day. They saw the man kidnapping Brooklyn hit her and took aim. I don't think your sister should ever trade her luck for talent. The girls had done some research and mixed up lime gelatin and oatmeal in hopes they'd get to have some fun launching condoms filled with the nasty shit at targets they set up this afternoon. I suspect Callie is going to be pissed when she sees the mess they've made in her garden." Looking past the gathering of people, Cat noticed several of the statues set among the flowers had targets tapped to them.

"Damn, look at this! Holy hell, the girls have done me

proud." Abby Garrett's amused voice sounded from beside them, but Cat noticed her husbands were keeping her away from the mess in front of them.

"No, Love, stay right here. We don't want you traipsing through what has to be the most disgusting crime scene I've ever seen." The power of Kalen Black's angelic voice was something Catalina always believed should be studied and replicated by law enforcement. How easy it would be to interrogate prisoners if they could replicate the power of Kalen's voice.

"I know that look. Cooper, you better get your woman away from Kalen, she's getting that glassy-eyed look they all get until they develop an immunity." Logan Douglas's teasing tone made her laugh, and Abby rolled her eyes.

"Don't fall for it, Cat. It's smoke and mirrors. All that audio-seduction is the devil's work, no angel would be nearly this deliciously deviant." Abby jumped into Kalen's arms, making both men growl as she pressed kisses along his jawline.

"Geez, get a room." Cat was grateful Cooper broke the tension she'd felt watching the soft-porn show in front of her even though she was fairly certain Abby was making a deliberate attempt to distract her from worrying about Brooklyn... or at least that might have been how it started. Laughing to herself, Catalina felt her shoulders relax for the first time since she'd gotten the call Brooklyn was in trouble. Glancing at Cooper, she was surprised to see him studying her.

"So where to now, Princess?" What seemed like a simple question was anything but. There were so many ways to interpret the question, and the damnable man had set her up perfectly. She couldn't deny the explosive chemistry between them, and the sex was incendiary, but the traits that made them so good in the bedroom seemed like they'd be the same ones to torpedo a relationship out of it. Taking a deep breath and turning to face him, Cat decided to err on the side of the angels and assume he really was talking about work.

"I'm headed back home. I need to spend some time in my studio finishing up a couple of commission pieces I was working on when *this* came up. Thank heavens I was far enough ahead, I should still be able to make the deadlines. I'm..." she took a deep breath to steady her nerves. Cat wasn't used to revealing this much personal information, but damn it, she owed him this much. "I'm going to cut back on the other... well, the other side of my business. The drive isn't there for me like it once was, and that compromises everyone's safety."

The understanding she saw in his eyes wasn't what she'd expected. He wrapped his large hand around her wrist, tugging her behind a large tree. Cooper used just enough force to bring them chest to chest, then leaned down to kiss her. The gentle press of his lips against hers was pure seduction. Slipping his tongue deep into her mouth ramped things up to scorching between one breath and the next. Her entire body was lighting up from the inside, and somewhere, buried in the deep recesses of her mind, she knew this was a bad idea, but her brain was no longer calling the shots.

Cooper's hand slid under her short dress to cup her bare ass, and Cat couldn't hold her groan as a wave of heat crashed through her, making her knees shake. He must have felt her falter because before she could break away, Cat found herself lifted until her legs wrapped around him. The press of his rigid length against her sex sent a rush of moisture from her vagina to coat the lips of her labia. *Oh Lord, I'm going to leave a mark on his leathers.*

The spell was slowly broken by the sound of a throat clearing a few feet away. Without even looking, Catalina knew it was Austin. *I swear to God, this is getting fucking old.* It wasn't the first time her oldest brother had caught her in a compromising position, but she hoped like hell it was the last. Resting her forehead against Cooper's shoulder, hoping to hide the flush she could feel burning her face, Cat took a deep breath and waited.

"I know what you're thinking, Kitten, but I wasn't trying to embarrass you. Is and I are getting ready to cut out, and we'd like to say goodbye." She heard him hesitate but didn't say anything. She'd just wait him out. Long seconds later, he added, "Cooper, Ian said to tell you to answer your phone. Evidently, the Lamonts have been trying to get in touch with you and were desperate enough to send out a wide sweeping message." He'd used the pet name he'd called her since she was a kid, and he'd thought Cat was too grown-up when she'd always been so petite. Austin was the only one of her siblings who'd ever called her Kitten, and the sentiment brought tears to her eyes.

Cooper turned his back to Austin before letting her slide down until her feet were on solid ground. Tipping her chin back with his fingers, he pressed a soft kiss to her forehead. "Duty calls, Princess. I hope they've gotten a break in the child trafficking case we've been working on." He must have sensed she was starting to shut down because he frowned and shook his head. "Not this time, Princess. Whatever we started this past week, isn't finished. I'll call you as soon as I can. You know the routine, it may not be as quick as I'd like—but it will be as soon as I can do so safely."

He was right, she knew the routine all too well. Calling someone you cared about during an op endangered everybody, including the person you called. Sighing, she watched him turn, shake hands with Austin as her brother thanked him for his help, then he was gone. Sighing, she looked at her brother and grinned.

"This is getting to be a habit, big brother."

Chapter Twenty-Five

BROOKLYN SAGGED BACK against the cracked leather chair in Detective Tucker's office. He sat across from her, but the small office was crammed with men and women from so many alphabet agencies, she'd lost count. She fought the urge to roll her eyes as he studied her with an intensity law enforcement usually reserved for perps, not victims.

There wasn't a chance in hell she was going to tell him why Mendoza had targeted her... and they both knew it. Luke had already warned her the man was a member of the club and knew all the details of the case, but that didn't mean she had to cop to everything in front of a damned firing squad. Quinn Tucker was six-four and solidly built; the retrieval expert in her would have made a number of mental notes about him between one heartbeat and the next. Detective Tucker would be impossible to dismiss, but she already knew his no-nonsense appearance hid a killer sense of humor... not that she planned to test it... but it was good to know.

She'd already been assured they had enough to convict both men. And if the information coming together about the intended use for the resort he was building turned out to be true, he'd spend the rest of his life behind bars, so why was he so intent on asking questions about Mendoza's motive?

He doesn't give a rat's ass, baby. He's simply doing what the FBI has asked him to do. Some of the players in the room you weren't introduced to would love to back you into a corner, then offer you a saving grace. Luke's voice floated through her mind, and she struggled to hold back her smile. She was finally getting more accustomed to telepathic communication and had to admit, it was damned handy at times.

Let me guess... they want me to work for them. She felt rather than heard his agreement and wanted to shake her head. Job offers had poured in during the days after the incident at the club. The insurance company she'd been working for was begging her to do *one more job,* even going so far as to pay her a two-million-dollar incentive. The only offer she'd accepted was Ian's. Brooklyn was thrilled to work with one of the most sought-after entrepreneurs in the world and even more thrilled she could do most of the work remotely.

"You're sure you have nothing to add, Ms. Adler? It seems odd for a man of Mr. Mendoza's reputation to target a woman at random." And there it was, the spark of humor in Detective Tucker's deep blue eyes that all but shouted his amusement.

"Can't think of anything I'd like to add, Detective. I think the evidence of Mendoza's mental instability is fairly well established. His schizophrenia diagnosis alone explains a lot." She hadn't lied. It did explain a lot. It just didn't explain *this*. He gave her an almost imperceptible nod, and she took the hint and stood. "Well, it's been interesting, but I've got a plane to catch. You have my contact information." Limping to where Luke stood leaning against the large window looking out over the department's atrium, all Brooklyn wanted to do was be on their way.

You read my mind, baby. Let's go, New Mexico awaits.

The End

Epilogue

S TANDING IN FRONT of one of several walls of glass in the mountain retreat Luke called a cabin, Brooklyn looked out over the vista. The view never ceased to steal her breath. New Mexico's claim as *The Land of Enchantment* was more than a turn of phrase for tourists… it was a fact. The deep hues of purple and blue coloring the sky as the sun set on another day danced across the sky, making her wonder at the simple beauty painted against some of the most specular scenery in the world.

Strong arms encircled her, pulling her back against Luke's bare chest. Without turning, Brooklyn knew he'd only dressed in the faded jeans he'd shed in haste a few hours ago. She'd stolen his button-down shirt… the one she'd been unbuttoning for him when he'd ripped the front placket apart, sending the last three buttons skittering across the floor. Giving herself a mental slap, she had to admit she'd been purposely goading him by moving at a torturously slow pace.

"You love to test my patience, don't you?"

The teasing tone in his voice made her smile. She was still counting her blessings. Not only had their relationship morphed from best friends to lovers with very few bumps in the road, Luke was helping her in ways she'd never imagined. He'd listened to her for hours as she weighed the various employment offers she'd received, asking questions that forced her to look at every angle until she could form her own conclusions. His unwavering support had deepened their bond, and she often worried she wasn't expressing how truly grateful she was. Turning her in his arms to look into her misty eyes, Luke pressed a soft kiss against her forehead.

"I love you, Brooklyn. Everything I do for you is because I want what's best for you, I don't expect you to make a big production of being grateful. There will come a time when you're the one guiding me through a tough time, and I'll be equally grateful because that's what love does." His sweet, heartfelt words were all it took to send the tears burning the backs of her eyes racing down her cheeks.

"The past six weeks have been the best in my life, Luke. Everything. The house is amazing. You've suffered through all my cursing during rehab with minimal *complaints*." She wasn't going to mention the spankings her cursing had earned because anything leading to mind-blowing orgasms couldn't really be called punishment. "Knowing you've gone to the incredible expense of providing a space for my family to visit, the media room set up for remote teaching... hell, all of it." She swept her hand around to encompass the enormous structure he'd built. Brooklyn never want to leave this space.

"I don't want you to ever leave, B. This was a labor of love—an investment in the future I've seen for us since we were freshmen at MIT. All the money in the world is useless if you can't use it to make life better for those you love. Seeing you standing here, looking out at the beauty wrapping around us, knowing how connected you feel to this place was the most erotic thing I've ever seen. The backlight showing off your naked body hidden only by my shirt made me want to open the front, press your warm breasts against the cool glass and fuck you from behind until neither of us could walk further than the leather sofa. I assure you, there is a reason it has a soft quilt draped over the back, and the remote for the fireplace is close at hand." She wanted to laugh at his casual description of the huge piece of furniture as a sofa. It was longer than two beds and wide enough for them to lay side-by-side.

Feeling a sudden jolt of electricity surge through her, Brooklyn found herself pitching forward against his chest as her knees folded out from under her. Blinding fear flooded her mind, and she felt as if she'd been transported to the scene rather than watching it from a distance. Brooklyn felt the moment her sister sensed her presence, but she had no idea how to explain what was happening. In the end, it didn't matter, there was no time for an explanation when a shot rang out, shattering a half-wall of glass behind her sister's shoulder.

"Oh, God. Oh, God. Oh, God." Brooklyn's whispered words were the last thing she remembered before the world around her swirled into darkness.

LUKE COULD SENSE everything Brooklyn was thinking, but not being able to see what she was seeing was frustrating as hell. To his knowledge, she'd never connected telepathically with anyone other than him, but even without talking to her, Luke knew what she was experiencing was frightening. Her mother had alluded to this, but he hadn't questioned her because their time that last morning was so limited. Now he wished he'd taken the extra time so he wouldn't feel so damned helpless now.

He'd felt compelled to connect with Brooklyn when she was running on empty and planning to take on one last, dangerous job. The compulsion had been so overwhelming, it had taken him several minutes to sort through everything bombarding him, his knees nearly folding out from under him as Brooklyn's had.

He made a mental note to call Taz Ledek and request he set up a meeting with his Lakota grandmother. Onatah Ledek was a gifted healer and one of the few still teaching. Luke knew her wisdom was being passed down, but he also realized someday she would no longer be available, and he wanted to learn all he could about his and Brooklyn's gifts while he could.

Feeling her tremble in his arms, Luke didn't hesitate to carry her to the living room so he could settle her on his lap. Maintaining a close physical connection would anchor her during the storm.

Brooklyn's whispered, "Oh, God. Oh, God. Oh, God," caused goose flesh to spread over his arms and the hair on the back of his neck stood up on end. Whatever she was seeing was terrifying her. The trembling woman in his arms didn't seem to be frightened for her own safety—she appeared to instinctively know she was an observer rather than a participant in the scene.

Luke's connection to Brooklyn faltered for a split second when she slipped into a semi-conscious state, but by focusing more fully on the link between them, he was able to bridge the gap. Realizing the ear-piercing noise he'd heard was gunfire kicked up his heart rate, matching Brooklyn's racing pulse. Danger and gunfire could only mean one woman in Brooklyn's inner circle—Catalina.

Catching fleeting glimpses of the scene proved almost impossible to piece together, but Luke tried to catalog all the mental images, hoping he and Brooklyn would be able to sort it all out later. The one element that stood out the most was the medicinal smell, not perfectly clean, but more like a laboratory—the realization had no soon drifted through his mind than Brooklyn began struggling in his arms. Flailing her arms and kicking with surprising strength, he was hard-pressed to keep her from falling.

"London, no!" Brooklyn's broken cry was part warning, part pleading, and a whole lot of fear. She fell back against him, completely spent, but he didn't have time to work through everything before his phone began vibrating in his pocket. Checking the caller I.D. didn't reveal anyone he'd expected although perhaps he should have. Dr. Evan Monroe's name was displayed prominently on the screen.

Books by Avery Gale

The ShadowDance Club
Katarina's Return – Book One
Jenna's Submission – Book Two
Rissa's Recovery – Book Three
Trace & Tori – Book Four
Reborn as Bree – Book Five
Red Clouds Dancing – Book Six
Perfect Picture – Book Seven

Club Isola
Capturing Callie – Book One
Healing Holly – Book Two
Claiming Abby – Book Three

Masters of the Prairie Winds Club
Out of the Storm
Saving Grace
Jen's Journey
Bound Treasure
Punishing for Pleasure
Accidental Trifecta
Missionary Position
Another Second Chance
Star-Crossed Miracles
Dusted Star
Lilly's Choice

The Wolf Pack Series
Mated – Book One
Fated Magic – Book Two
Tempted by Darkness – Book Three

The Knights of the Boardroom
Book One
Book Two
Book Three

The Morgan Brothers of Montana
Coral Hearts – Book One
Dancing with Deception – Book Two
Caged Songbird – Book Three
Game On – Book Four
Well Bred – Book Five

Mountain Mastery
Well Written
Savannah's Sentinel
Sheltering Reagan

Enchanted Holidays
The Christmas Painting

The Adlers
Brooklyn

I would love to hear from you!

Website:
www.averygale.com

Facebook:
facebook.com/avery.gale.3

Twitter:
@avery_gale

www.ingramcontent.com/pod-product-compliance
Lightning Source LLC
Chambersburg PA
CBHW060924180626
46817CB00004B/1390